Murder Unedited

A Will Deas Mystery

By

Ian Stout

Fifeshire Press
Toronto Ontario Canada

Published by Fifeshire Press

5 Parnell Avenue, Toronto Ontario Canada M1K-1B1

www.Fifeshirepress.com

First Edition July 2015

Cover and text design: Rajai Sawalha of Print Express

ISBN: 978-0-9878648-3-3

Cataloging data available from Library and Archives Canada

Printed and bound in the United States of America

The characters and events in this book are fictitious. Any similarity to real persons, either living or dead, is coincidental and not intended by the author. This is a work of fiction and the people herein are the product of the author's rather wild imagination.

Acknowledgments

My thanks go out to the following people:

Members of the Peel Regional Police Department at the Erin Mills Parkway Station who never seemed to tire of my questions regarding police procedures.

William G. Stout, retired teacher, business operator and brother. Michael Sinelnikoff, actor, director, producer and writer. Nancy Provan-Jones, a proud Scot and diligent proofreader, and Rajai Sawalha, owner of Print Express, who knows how to make what I write look good.

Richard Philpot, retired computer whiz, for guidance in computer matters and his wife Sandy who knows word processing inside out.

Deserving special thanks is Sharon Stout, who read the book so many times she's probably able to recite it word for word. All writers should have a spouse like my Sharon.

A Note from the Author

At the launch party for my second novel, *Necessary Tourist*, we held a draw with the winner having the right to a fictional role in my next book.

The rules were simple. The winner had to agree to be in the book and would have to sign a release. They could read those sections of the story they were part of and would be allowed to make suggestions. They also had the right to opt out any time before printing.

Approximately one hundred and twenty names went into the bowl and the lucky person was Mr. Winston Rhule, my next door neighbor of more than twenty years. We were both delighted with this result and I happily made him a writer of children's books.

My wife Sharon suggested this fun idea and we have now done it twice. We will definitely be doing it again.

Murder Unedited

Chapter One

Michael hated being disturbed during a creative moment and glared with distaste at the phone before abandoning his keyboard to answer.

"Hello" he growled, not knowing who was at the other end.

"Hello Michael darling. Hello, hello, hello my darling Michael." chirped a happy voice. "Have you heard the news? I hope not, because I want to be the one to tell you. Oh God! Do I have news for you and I'm so happy to deliver it. You'll never believe it. You'll never, ever believe it. Our own 'piss poor publisher' is dead, deader than a doorknob."

There was no mistaking the joy in the high-pitched excited voice of the caller.

"That's 'doornail' Rosanne, 'dead as a doornail.' My God, have you never read Henry the Sixth or any Dickens? It's a doornail my dear, but that doesn't matter, just stop fooling around. You're being silly and I'm very busy and there's no way in hell I could have such good fortune. I'll never outlive that dishonest little snot."

"Michael, I'm not kidding, this is no joke. He was found on his back in an alley behind one of those watering holes he spent his time supporting. He bore all the earmarks of a bona-fide one hundred percent dead person." Rosanne's almost hysterical glee washed over Michael like a tidal wave.

3

She continued "He had no pulse, he wasn't breathing, and you just have to hear this; you won't believe it! He wasn't screwing some poor writer out of all his hard earned money! To top it off, when someone offered to buy him a drink, there was no response, can you imagine that, no response! There is no question about it my dear. Peter, our piss poor publisher, is well and truly dead."

"Are you sure about all this?" a still skeptical Michael asked.

"Of course I'm sure, you silly. It's on TV, radio and the front page of our local paper which has that horrid picture taken of him at last summer's book-fest. You know the one, when he got drunk and insulted poor Margaret Atwood."

"Hang on then" a completely changed and delighted Michael instructed his caller. "I've got a bottle of champagne just for something like this. It's been waiting for a momentous event and by God this certainly meets all the criteria" and setting the phone down, he heaved himself out of his chair and shuffled off to fetch the bottle from the wine fridge in the pantry of his tiny Montreal apartment.

Returning with two glasses, he balanced the phone on his shoulder while undoing the wire and easing out the cork, all the while chattering cheerily into Rosanne's ear.

"Dear Rosanne, do tell me the wonderful details and leave nothing out and please don't tell me it was sudden. You know what I mean. Nothing like a crass quick gunshot to the head or a large blade thrust straight through his black heart. It's important the little bastard suffered."

Michael was bouncing in his chair with joy. "By the way, I have two glasses, one for you and one for me. I can't celebrate this stroke of good fortune alone, you know, it just wouldn't do. Of course, I'll have to drink yours for you but you can pretend, although you're not missing much. It is French but not a very good year" and he downed both flutes before setting them beside the phone for refilling, all the while humming a happy tune.

Michael Kalishnikoff, who loved champagne and horse racing in that order, claimed to be an Englishman sired by two well-bred members of pre-revolution Russian nobility. His parents were amongst those who had the good sense to escape the motherland shortly after the Reds moved the whole Romanov family to a place called Yekaterinburg. Michael's father, not a stupid man, bribed a ship's captain with a handful of gold coins, and moved lock, stock and family from St. Petersburg to London. Tucked carefully into his wife Katrina's hair and stowed in bags hidden beneath her floor length dress were most of the family jewels, several kilos of gold coins, and a small fortune in British five pound notes.

Looking much like a sickly woman barely able to walk and leaning heavily on the arm of her husband,

Mrs. Kalishnikoff and her crafty husband managed to sneak out enough of the family fortune to acquire a splendid home in Kensington. They also had enough left over to maintain a reasonably upper class life-style for the next four decades.

As those years passed, additions to the brood completed the stable of twelve Kalishnikoffs, with Michael the last in 1935. He always claimed he was the best because his parents finally got it right after so much practice.

Those early times were a blur of laughter, boating and croquet on the lawn with older siblings. Michael quickly learned being the youngest and the cutest afforded him a distinct advantage and the little mischief-maker was quite the favorite of his aging father. Shortly after the war broke out in 1939 he was shipped to a relative's home in Canada where he continued to win the hearts of all he encountered.

To this day, more than sixty years later, he still thought he was cute, and actually, sitting there with a champagne bottle resting against his ample stomach and the phone nestled in his perfectly trimmed beard, he did looked like an impish Santa Claus happily taking orders for toys.

As the warmth of the champagne spread through him, Michael peppered his caller with questions, eager for details.

"Rosanne, tell me my dear, what happened?"

"Well, I have the paper right here and the details are a little skimpy but it would seem someone killed him with, of all things, a fountain pen. Now if that's not poetic justice, nothing is. Can you possibly imagine a more fitting way to do in that little twerp? Oh God, life at times can be soooo good." Rosanne said sounding beyond being happy.

"A reporter on local TV said there was a lot of blood around the body so he must have lain there quite some time before going to the great 'remainder display table in the sky'. So yes, I'd think he may have suffered somewhat."

Rosanne Drew, like Michael, was a writer under contract to the victim, the infamous and much unloved Peter 'the piss poor publisher' Jefferson, founder and president of Crafty Press, a company known to many industry insiders as Crappy Press. Peter Jefferson was a man who had managed over the past two decades to alienate, aggravate and irritate every person with whom he came into contact, as well as many who were spared that misfortune.

Being the author of several very good childrens books, Rosanne was considered quite gifted by Toronto's literati, if that meant anything. None of them ever purchased books anyway but were useful if you could use their verbal pontificating on the back cover of your next effort. Besides writing skills, she was renowned as a genius for having coined the descriptive title of 'Peter, the piss poor publisher'.

This incredibly accurate description of Peter Jefferson was born after Crafty Press produced and distributed hundreds of Rosanne's second book to sellers across the land with her name misspelled in large letters across the front cover. Rosanne's first book had been a great success, selling more than three thousand copies nationwide, and Peter wanted to trade on her ability. The trouble was he didn't check the galleys as close as he should have.

Dismayed, the author demanded something be done but Peter callously dismissed her complaint. He said no one would notice an extra 'S' in her first name and snarled that he wouldn't waste money recovering the damn thing. When she demanded he recall the book, he told her to 'drop dead'.

Being under contract to Crafty Press 'for life' Peter bullied her into believing if she took any action her literary career would be over. One email from him claimed a two-bit hack like her would spend the rest of her days in court and she'd never publish another thing again, ever.

Rosanne backed down, defeated by his verbal abuse, retreating to her apartment to lick her wounds. No one heard from her for weeks.

When she finally emerged, having decided not to press the matter, Rosanne, with great dignity, refused to discuss the matter. She would just tolerate the screwed-up cover but she would never forgive Peter. From that day on, her publisher became 'Peter the piss poor publisher' usually spit out with a snarl. She also made sure everyone in the industry knew his new nickname and understood the reason for it.

"Do your local authorities have any idea who should get the credit for doing this?" Michael asked.

"The official line says it was a bungled robbery, possibly by someone who thought it an easy hit because the twit was so drunk. That cheap fake Rolex he wore was gone. His wallet was gone along with all his maxed out credit cards. There was no cash on him, although the cheap little bastard never did have any when he was out, so if they're right and it was robbery, it was by the world's dumbest thief. He was a first class bungler not knowing his victim was such a penniless loser" she spat.

"Gracious me, you say our esteemed publisher was under the influence? You mean Peter had been touching the demon rum? I'm shocked, shocked. The police should check the bar to see who was paying" Michael laughed.

"Good idea. I'll suggest they find the payee when they call, as I'm sure they will." Both Rosanne and Michael had a good chuckle over this because Peter's love of booze, any booze, was legend around the publishing world, especially when it was free and served by some young beauty with long legs.

Michael's mind was churning but he was pleased at this apparent change in his career. He too was under a 'for life' contract with Crafty Press and this news was possibly life changing.

"It's so good of you to call with this wonderful news. I feel as though I've just won the grand prize in a lottery. I assume you'll be seeking a new publisher, as indeed I will. Please do keep me up to date on your efforts and any further developments in this heartwarming saga," he said.

"I've already sent out feelers as I'm sure all of us will, and of course I'll keep you up to date. I knew you felt the same about him as I did but I never thought he was in your champagne category. You owe me, you know" and she laughed like she did years ago at a book launch in Toronto.

"I'll always owe you, my dear. I owe you because a long time ago you decided I was to be a member of your small circle of close friends. For that, I'll always owe you."

"Damn, Michael, you sure haven't lost the ability to sweet talk me" Rosanne said before hanging up.

Chapter Two

Detective Will Deas used his shoulder to push the heavy door of Police Headquarters open so his short, somewhat overweight frame could make its way through. He wearily nodded to a couple from drugs heading the other way because his arms were full of files and papers on the last case he worked. He was tired, having been up all night finishing off reports needed by his boss Collin Fraser, head of homicide, and Herman Duchek, the Crown Prosecutor.

His old bones, having done the same thing for thirty-five years, somehow knew only six more were left before retirement and six months each year in the Florida sun. But until that day arrived the rumpled suit of Detective Will Deas along with his weary bones and sore eyes would continue to be the best Hamilton had.

He became a cop after being laid off as a burner in the flat-plate rolling mill of Dominion Foundries and Steel in Hamilton. At that time his pretty wife was pregnant with their first child and due in less than six weeks. His apartment's rent of a hundred and fifty dollars was due in two weeks and his pogey, as unemployment insurance was called, was due when the government decided to send his first cheque. The young Will Deas knew Dofasco was the best steel mill in the world to work but waiting for a call-back wasn't an option. There was no doubt he needed a job with a secure pay cheque right away, so he started looking.

Will soon discovered his city was looking for new policemen. Recruits had to meet a preset standard in intelligence, physical fitness and have the ability to handle themselves in the gritty back alleys of a tough steel town. Will Deas, only a few years out of the Gorbals of Glasgow, knew how to survive on mean streets better than most and decided the city needed him.

He breezed through the initial tests, was accepted and entered their training program. Throwing himself into the schedule he did well and his instructors noted the young Scot as one to watch. Six months later, with his again pregnant wife watching proudly with their young son in her arms, Will Deas was sworn in with eleven other new policemen and his long march to being Hamilton's foremost detective began.

Assigned to a beat in the notorious north end of Hamilton, Will the rookie was soon walking down James Street beside a huge grizzled old cop who towered over Will's five foot nine inch frame.

This partner, who at first scared the hell out of Will, was one Constable First Class Patrick Ryan, nearing sixty and as Irish as Paddy's pig. PC Ryan knew more about human nature, policing, and the needs and desires of those he policed better than anyone the rookie ever met, before or since.

Will's next seven years pounding the streets beside his tough old partner was like a continuous university course in human nature and deviant behavior. As an added extra, Will received a first-hand education in all the non-police problems' citizens ran into every day. He understood the pain of a mother of three whose husband dropped dead of a heart attack. He saw the hunger in the faces of children when the breadwinner of the family was on strike. He also learned of the anguish of a young girl whose fiancé was arrested for some minor criminal act.

Will saw, but never mentioned, his partner dipping into his own pocket to slip a dollar or two into the hand of someone down on his luck, shooing them away when they tried to thank him. He grew in many ways during those years with PC Ryan. Will became wiser, more understanding and learned to tolerate the idiosyncrasies of the world around him.

During that time the brass were taking note of his work and when Patrick Ryan retired they moved Will to the investigators division. They knew what they were doing because Will Deas developed into the best damn detective on the Hamilton Police Force.

"Collin wants to see you" called the Desk Sergeant as Will came through the door. The Sergeant didn't bother raising his head or taking his eyes off his morning paper because he knew from a distance the smell of Will's pipe. It wasn't just any pipe. It was an ancient toxic briar always stuffed with Gallaher's Irish Plug. Though tucked into a pocket of Will's jacket, the acrid smell of the coarse black tobacco clung to him and announced his presence to anyone within twenty feet. Most considered the aroma of his pipe a great stink.

"Gotcha" Will called back and turned to his right.

Collin Fraser was Chief of Detectives and would someday be chief of the whole place. About six foot two with a handsome square face and a charming smile, he moved about the community making speeches at service clubs and schools. If he hadn't become a cop he would have made a great politician. Everyone believed he would be the next Chief and Will thought about that as he rapped on Collin's door before pushing it open.

"What's up?" he asked of the man behind the desk.

"The Dundas killing" Collin said, waving Will toward a seat. "The one on the morning news, I'm sure you heard. Nothing much gets by you."

"You mean the drunk in the alley behind the bar? Sure, I heard. It sounded rather routine."

"Probably is" Collin said and set aside some papers to give Will his full attention. "It appears to be an old fashioned mugging that went sour but you know the Dundas crowd. All those Foo-Foo people hiding in their million dollar homes need a little hand holding. The mayor wants a show of the old 'There's nothing to worry about' and maybe a little of the 'It's an isolated incident' thrown in. I'm having a press conference in an hour to announce that we're assigning our best detective to the case and I'll tell them he's working on it as we speak. You're in charge and this should be wrapped up very quickly." Collin smiled at Will with no humor.

"I wish you had warned me. I would have put on a clean shirt and shined my shoes."

"Don't worry," Collin laughed genuinely. "I doubt anyone would notice. Clean shirt, shiny shoes, even a brush through your mop would make no difference, you'd still smell like an old outhouse".

"Do you need me at the announcement?"

"No, you're not up to speed yet so best you be scarce. I'll say you were assigned early this morning, which you were, and you're working hard studying the evidence we've collected."

"Go see Ford in forensics and get what he has, then check with Davidson. He was chief uniform at the scene last night and did the file. He'll be happy to turn it over. When you collect it all, go home. I want you to stay away until you're up and running and able to do your own press conference, now on your way" and he waved Will out of the office.

Leaving with a fake groan Will headed toward forensics. He smiled at the idea of spending the rest of the day lounging near his pool with his old cat Sherlock and a dram or two of his favorite amber liquid close at hand. It certainly beat working.

Chapter Three

The autopsy report lying on Fred Ford's stainless steel work table was unadorned with fancy medical phrases and like Fred, spoke to Will in layman's terms. Death occurred between one and two a.m. after the victim was hit from behind on the left back section of his head. He fell sideways and backwards onto his right side. The blow was hard enough to knock him out, but not hard enough to kill him, meaning he was simply unconscious when he hit the ground. There was a tiny laceration on his right wrist and fragments of glass were found under his right hand. A mark on that wrist indicated a watchband but no watch was found.

Fred's untechnical phrase for the cause of death was 'he bled to death' because of a puncture wound in the main artery in his neck as he lay unconscious on the pavement.

Will asked what caused the puncture and Fred, looking over his reading glasses with a wry face, held up a plastic evidence bag containing a blue fountain pen with gold colored bands and clip.

"This fountain pen, a rather cheap one, I might suggest. Probably put together by some overworked and underpaid peasant in a drab village in that paradise called the People's Republic of China. I would hope if someone intended to kill me with a pen they'd have enough decency and class to use a Mont

Blanc or one of the better Waterman's, but this; tacky, very tacky."

"Was it his?" Will asked, squinting through the bag at the pen.

"I would think so. How often have you seen a thug clutching a cheap fountain pen wandering the streets of our fair city in search of his next victim? Besides, everything about our victim is third class. His jeans, shoes, shirt, even his faux Harris Tweed jacket, complete with genuine imitation leather elbow pads, they're all knock-offs. Yes, I'd say there's a good chance the pen was his." Fred took the bag from Will's hand and dropped it on top of several others containing assorted items.

"Odd" Will mused "whoever did the nasty deed stopped, took the cap off, possibly to see if it was worth anything, and then jammed it into his neck. Where was the cap?"

"Lying on the right side of the body, about three feet away, flipped there by the killer. You're right though. Why would our killer remove the cap while searching his victim for something valuable? You'd think he'd just pocket it. Of course the victim was a publisher, perhaps the killer was going to write a novel."

"Is that a wee bit of coroner's humor?" Will asked, raising one bushy eyebrow.

Over the years Will had seen a lot of different and sometimes ingenious weapons used to kill people but this was a new one. He was sure the pen was mightier than the sword but he didn't think that jamming one into a drunk's jugular vein was quite what was meant by that expression.

Forensic files underarm, Will strolled to Sergeant Davidson's office to grab his 'senior at the scene' investigator's report. He left the building twenty-five minutes later lugging his bundle of reports and papers, quite happy he was missing Collin's news conference, stopping only for a moment in the parking lot to light his old briar.

Nodding to a couple of arriving reporters while unlocking his car he silently thanked heaven for not having to stay and face them. He had a lot to go through, including half a bottle of Teacher's, and he looked forward to the peace and quiet the rest of the day offered.

The case Collin handed Will was a routine botched mugging but because it occurred in the wealthy residential enclave of Dundas it would require a delicate hand. The Mayor's beautiful home nestled nearby along with much of Hamilton's wealth, and Will knew appearances would be important. This was an investigation needing sensitivity.

Those living in that high-end section of the city were the movers and shakers of Hamilton. They were constantly mixing at cocktail parties and backyard Bar-B-Q's and all had the private phone numbers on their speed dials of the local political leaders and other important officials. Will knew some of those people and he knew they'd be contacting him so he'd better be sure he had all the details in place.

Sitting beside his pool and going through his files Will thought about Fred's wry comments on how the victim's blood alcohol level indicated a man in serious training for the booze guzzling Olympics. The forensic specialist figured that if the victim had not been found for three months his body would still be preserved in perfect condition.

He had little in his stomach other than hard liquor and beer, meaning no dinner. The witness notes on the bar waitress said he was a regular and was sitting alone in a corner with a boiler-maker in hand when she started at five. Knowing him to be a surly drunk she just left him alone, refilling his glass only when he waved.

No wallet was found. There was no loose change, nor a phone book or Blackberry. In fact he had nothing. There wasn't a scrap of paper, no receipt of any kind or even a handkerchief. The killer had taken a lot of time and was very thorough. Other than his clothing, the victim left this world with only a pen in his possession and that was firmly stuck in his neck.

The file showed Jefferson's car keys to be missing but indicated his locked car was parked just fifty feet away. Will considered Mothers Against Drunk Drivers might have killed Peter Jefferson to keep him off the road but it didn't seem likely. He had heard nothing of them changing tactics lately so with a sigh he discarded MADD as a possible suspect. At that moment the phone beside him on his patio rang.

"Deas here" he answered.

"Hi Will, it's Collin. Have you gone over the Jefferson material yet?"

"Just done a quick look through and sitting here thinking about it. There's a few things that might be unusual but really, it seems to be just an everyday run of the mill mugging gone sour. Some thug bopped him and took their time going through his pockets stealing everything the guy had. I'd say the asshole took so long looking for something of value the victim started to come around. Our thief panicked, was holding the pen when the drunk started to move and blindly swung at him. A good lawyer would plead involuntary manslaughter." Will stopped to sip from his glass before continuing.

"I think we should be looking for someone about as tall as Mr. Jefferson because the blow that knocked him out was coming in a straight line and hit him on the back of his head, I'd say about five feet six. I would also think he was unemployed or into drugs because he was looking for anything and everything he could sell or pawn, so we'll start checking the pawnshops for a wristwatch, possibly with a cracked or broken lens."

Collin seriously said "You may be right and we'll go with that scenario officially, but I want you to do a little more digging into Mr. Jefferson's lifestyle. I think there may be more to this than meets the eye." Will took his lead from his boss's tone.

"What have you got?"

"Not that much, but you know what instincts are. You hear something and the hair on the back of your neck starts to bristle. You know what I mean." Collin paused and Will could hear paper being shuffled around his superior's desk. After a few seconds he heard Collin mutter something profane then his voice came through clearly.

"First off" Collin continued, "a grinning reporter asked if we expected anyone other than the victim's immediate family at the funeral. I wasn't quite sure what he meant but his comment prompted snickers and grins throughout the gathering. After the press conference I poked about and it seems our victim, who by the way spent twenty years as a newspaper reporter, was not the best liked person in the literary industry. In fact, it might be more accurate to say he was pretty well despised by all who knew him.

"A couple of uniforms in the west end of town have some history with Mr. Jefferson and they considered him a rather nasty piece of work. One of them, Tony Valeriano, you know him, once said the next time he had to deal with the little jerk it wouldn't be a ride home to his wife, but a night in the slammer. Tony said he'd had enough of his foul mouth and abuse and calls him a mean, bad tempered drunk." Will noted Tony Valeriano's name for future use as Collin paused for a moment. "I also called Kristy down at records in the Court House and she knows Mr. Jefferson well. There's a small claims lawsuit in progress right now for twenty-five large brought by one of his authors. He also has an eight hundred thousand dollar suit sitting in Toronto's Superior Court alleging he libeled another author. It's pending, awaiting an examination for discovery. There's another floating around by an author in Brampton.

"On top of all that, there's been an inquiry from a very large and very expensive Bay Street law firm representing a bookstore chain. That one has something to do with returns and I don't know quite what that means so you might check that out too. All in all I think this guy had big troubles and a closer look is called for." Collin's tone changed.

"Now that I've done all the hard work, go tie up the loose ends and you can do the next news conference so you can get all the credit."

Will knew this last was said with an ear to ear grin across Collin's face.

"Thank you noble Laird of the police world" Will groveled in his put-on brogue. "These precious wee crumbs you toss me are much appreciated. I'd be right daft not to follow up on your wise counsel." Both men were laughing as the call ended.

Will sat quietly thinking about the call, gently stroking the soft black and white coat of Sherlock who lay contentedly in his lap. The purring of his companion - a kitten when picked up at the SPCA a month after his wife moved out - helped his thought processes. Finally he reached for his phone once again. It was time to track down his partner Lou Shatz, the world's worst golfer.

Off for the day taking a break after fifteen straight shifts cleaning up two cases, Lou was probably out on a golf course trying to kill a poor ball.

Lou's day off was why Collin suggested Will take time to go over the details. Collin knew his best detective would never take a day off no matter how long he had gone without a break. It had something to do with Will's damned stubborn Scottish background and his ancient and archaic work ethic. The only way Collin could get him to relax even a bit was by having him review a case at home beside his pool with a bottle of Scotch.

Collin's plan worked. Will had a mellow glow after a couple of drinks but his mind was still working at full speed around the details of the case. He was making plans for the next day and waiting for the call from Lou. He knew it would come.

Chapter Four

Lou, impeccably dressed as was his manner, sat at his desk in homicide an hour before Will rolled in, methodically going over all five papers that carried news of the Hamilton area. He was checking their take on the murder of the local businessman.

The Hamilton Spectator, as one might expect, had front page coverage. The National Post, Globe and Mail, the Sun and the Star, all based in Toronto, covered the killing adequately on pages three or four of their first sections. Only the Spec tended to show any sympathy but it was directed toward the widow, not the victim. Lou made note of that.

Will stopped by to suggest they get a coffee and go over plans for the day. Lou wanted to know who was buying and when Will said he was, the younger man bounced to his feet, muttering some nonsense about losing a bundle playing Nassau on the golf course.

Will just shook his head and turned toward the machines. His frugal Scottish background prevented him from understanding why a golfer as bad as Lou would wager on himself. It was like a fat ninety year old one legged man competing in a marathon and betting he would win.

"Collin wants us to give this thing a good going over. He has a feeling it may be a bit more than a simple botched mugging, plus he has to throw a bone to the City Hall suits. I thought about this yesterday and besides looking amongst the usual gang of low-life's and problem people, maybe we should get ourselves a list of our victim's friends and business associates, let's spend some time questioning them. You never know, there may be more here than meets the eye and it will make our investigation look pretty thorough." Will took a sip of coffee, made a disgusting face and waited for Lou's answer.

"I can understand why he feels funny about this one. I went through the papers and the one thing that struck me was how no one, not one single reporter, had a good word to say about the victim. There's nothing bad mind you, but it was carefully neutral. Here's an example" and Lou rummaged through his pile, pulling out a section of the Star. Flipping the pages he found what he wanted.

"Listen to this, and I quote, 'the victim was found about two A.M. by a staff member of the bar Mr. Jefferson had been in for the previous five or six hours. Bar staff confirmed Mr. Jefferson, a regular customer, had been alone all evening and had been drinking heavily.' I'm shocked that a reporter would suggest one of their own might drink heavily" Lou finished with a broad grin.

Will smiled without humor. "Talk about people in glass houses. It is the first time I've ever seen that."

Lou continued "According to all reports this guy wasn't a member of the local literary landscape. He never attended any of their charitable soirees. He didn't contribute to worthy causes. He was never seen at a fund raising event and he never sponsored a little league baseball or hockey team. He was definitely not the epitome of a good corporate or even private citizen. I've gone through every story and I get the feeling there are few people who are sorry he's gone." Lou said and sat back, finishing his coffee with a satisfied grin.

"Well let's get started." Will said as he consulted his notebook, ticking off things as he spoke. "Call his wife and see if we can set up an interview with her today. Maybe she can tell us if there was anyone sorry he's gone. You got her number?"

Lou called, and when Vivienne Jefferson answered he was a little taken aback by her calm and collected manner on the phone. It had been little more than twenty-four hours since her husband's brutal murder and if she was upset, she sure didn't indicate it during their phone conversation. An interview time was set for two hours hence and the two detectives adjourned to Will's office to plan their visit.

Will gave Lou a brief rundown on the details passed to him by Collin plus a couple others he had managed to dig up. The more he studied the background and character of their corpse, the less he thought it was a robbery. His years on the force taught him to trust his instincts and Will's sixth sense suggested the killer had gone to a lot of trouble making it look like a robbery, but maybe just a little too much trouble. It was all a bit too perfect.

First off, the officers at the scene could not find anything used to belt the deceased over the head. The coroner said he wasn't sure yet what the attacker used but it wasn't sharp or jagged. No skin was broken, just flattened and bruised from the blow suggesting something like a two by four but there were no wood fragments or slivers in the hair or anywhere near on the ground. Further tests would have to be done to narrow down what kind of blunt weapon was used. It was strange the assailant would bring a weapon then carry it away when finished.

"Another strange thing Lou, why did he take the car keys but not the car? Valeriano searched the area thoroughly and there were no keys. Did the killer have his own car or did he walk away?" Neither had an answer for that one.

While waiting to leave for the widow's home Will asked his partner to get all the details on the lawsuits pending with names, law firms and those litigants involved. He was wondering who was spending all the dough to sue some small publisher in an industry filled with stories of financial failure. It could lead to something interesting. After all, he thought, one should always follow the money.

He had also asked records to do a deep check of the victim, his wife and the company. A call was put into the Ontario Provincial Police, the RCMP plus

Customs and Immigration. One never knew what might pop up, where Mr. Jefferson may have been, and what his movements were.

It would take a day or two to collect that information but it didn't matter. Peter Jefferson wasn't going anywhere for a while and the killer might think they'd gotten away with it. All would work out.

Will Deas and Lou Shatz strolled out to the parking lot an hour later discussing Canada's great passion, hockey. As always the prospects of the Toronto team's chances came up because it was the closest to Hamilton. The Leaf's past season had been a stinker and they were predicting how the next one might turn out. Before reaching the car a new ten dollar bet was made. Lou, ever the optimist, said the team would make the first round of playoffs. Will, more realistic, put up his cash feeling safe they wouldn't. There was no discussion of the team winning the Stanley Cup.

Chapter Five

Walking up the driveway of the widow Jefferson's home both detectives took note of the rundown condition of the entire place. Although a beautiful structure similar to most homes in this swank Dundas section of Hamilton, the owner obviously didn't have the money to keep it in repair or simply didn't give a damn how it looked.

The lawn hadn't seen a mower in weeks but considering the weeds outnumbered the blades of grass by a ratio of five hundred to one, a lawnmower seemed rather useless.

The original paint on the double garage door was cracked and peeling away, giving the front an antiqued look. Rain gutters sagged in several places and in one spot appeared disconnected from the down spout. They, like the garage door, hadn't seen a paint brush in a decade or two.

A shutter from a front window was off, leaning forlornly against the house below its normal perch, adding to the overall air of neglect. As they reached the front door they turned to each other to exchange their 'problems in this place' looks.

Lou rang the doorbell and when they realized it didn't work. pulled open the screen door with its gaping tear in the bottom and rapped with authority. The door opened immediately and Vivienne

Jefferson, the personification of a weary, mid-forties suburban housewife, smiled politely at the two men.

"Yes, may I help you" she asked, pulling a worn black sweater closely around her slender shoulders and brushing aside an errant strand of dirty blonde hair from her forehead.

Will could see the remnants of a very beautiful woman standing in front of him and knew it was not just the death of her husband taking a toll. She was like the house, good bones but showing the signs of years of neglect.

The Mrs. Jefferson he and Lou were looking at wore no make-up on her perfectly structured face and had only halfheartedly run a brush through her hair. She didn't seem to care about her appearance and looked like the product of many years in a tough marriage.

Both detectives held their badge folders open and Will spoke first, "I'm Will Deas of the Hamilton Police Force and this is my partner Detective Lou Shatz. We called a couple of hours ago asking if we could have a few words with you."

"Oh yes" was all she said and held the door open, waving both men into a large but tattered open foyer dominated by a grand curved wooden staircase sweeping majestically up to the second floor. Mrs. Jefferson silently closed the door and stepped around them, gesturing to her right, ushering them into a large living room.

The house was big. Will figured in the thirty-five hundred square foot range. It was much like many upscale subdivision homes built across southern Ontario in the 1980's and 90's for up and coming young executives.

Two stories tall with four bedrooms and two baths up, while on the ground floor was a dining room, living room, kitchen and family room plus a small powder room. The mandatory two car garage and wide driveway dominated the front and the building took up a good two thirds of the lot area. Will had seen many like it but most were in much better condition.

The two detectives sat on the sofa as the slender Mrs. Jefferson sank into an ancient armchair across from them, making Will think she might disappear into its worn cushions. She didn't though, and when she ceased her downward slide she just sat with a blank stare, waiting for their questions. Will started.

"I want you to know how sorry we are for what happened to your husband the other night."

"Thank you," she said quietly and touched her handkerchief to her eye. Unlike her cool phone manner, she was now having trouble coping.

"My partner and I have been assigned to ferret out the person responsible for this tragedy and we hope you can give us some information to help us in the investigation. Do you think you can talk to us now or would you like us to come back later?"

"I'll try now" she said in no more than a whisper, both hands in her lap clutching her handkerchief.

"Thank you, we appreciate that" and Will opened his notebook.

"When did your husband go over to the bar?"

"I think about eight o'clock. He had come home about six thirty. He had been out at meetings all day long. I made him something to eat and we watched Jeopardy, it's one of our favorite shows and we try not to miss it. After that he decided he wanted to go for a beer. He does that occasionally."

"You say you prepared dinner for him?" Lou asked.

"I always do," she said vaguely.

"What did he have?"

"I'm not sure, let me think. The children and I had already eaten so I just warmed something up, it might have been a meat pie with bread and a beer."

Lou looked to Will who was making notes on his pad and decided not to pursue the matter.

"And what did you do after he left?" Will made notes while he spoke.

"I tidied up a bit for half an hour or so, found the book I had been reading, a submission by a new author, and took it to bed with me. I must have fallen asleep around eleven and slept until your officer knocked on the door." She looked directly into Will's eyes, trying to be strong and helpful.

"I'm truly sorry you had to get that kind of knock on your door" he said.

"Your people were very good to me. There was a lady officer with them and she was very kind. Please pass on my thanks to them."

Will said he would and shifted to details of her husband. "We believe it was a robbery, possibly by someone in the bar who saw him leave and followed him. We are also considering it could have been a wandering drug addict spotting an easy hit for some cash and it went wrong. Your husband appears to have been an innocent victim in the wrong place at the wrong time." He waited for this to sink in as he approached his next question.

"I must ask you another thing. Can you think of anyone who might want to take your husband's life?"

Mrs. Jefferson started, seemingly surprised.

"Do you mean plan this, and do it for some reason other than robbery?"

"Yes."

"Well Officer Deas, my husband was certainly not the easiest man in the world to get along with. He was a tough businessman who knew what he wanted and would never let anyone take advantage. There were people who may have not liked him, but kill him, no, we don't know anyone like that. His publishing business dealt with a better class of people, literary people you know." She was very emphatic.

"Can you tell me what keys he had along with his car keys?" Will asked.

Vivienne Jefferson thought for a moment before answering "he had a house key of course, in fact two, one for the front and one for the side door. He had a mailbox key and he had a key for my car."

Lou Shatz leaned forward with a suggestion. "If it was a thief and he has the brains to find the address of your home he may try to get in to steal something. I would strongly suggest getting your locks changed."

"Goodness, I never thought of that. Thank you so much. I'll take care of it immediately." She seemed truly appreciative.

Checking his notes Will asked "I'm sorry but I do have to ask one last question if I may. Since this is a home based business, would you have a list of those 'literary people' you mentioned? You know, the authors he dealt with, the list of book customers he had and the suppliers he dealt with. That would be a great help in getting this thing wrapped up."

The distraught woman considered the request then stood and said "Of course, I think I can pull up a list on Peter's desktop. The list may not be up to date so I'll check his papers and if I find any others I could e-mail them to you. Also, if you think it might help, I'll round up some of his latest books so you can see what Crafty Press publishes."

Lou and Will sat while Mrs. Jefferson disappeared through the kitchen to an office out of sight. The two men quietly looked around the room, noting the condition of the place.

The inexpensive carpet was faded and frayed at the edges, its pattern worn in places. Both men spotted lint and small dust bunnies across it, indicating she probably hadn't vacuumed when she tidied up the night her husband died. Will figured the carpet saw a vacuum as regularly as the lawn saw a mower.

The drapes across the wide front windows were sun faded and hung listlessly from a slightly bent rod. Even the sofa they sat on would have been rejected by Goodwill or the Salvation Army. Both men's eyes met and Lou rolled his upwards.

Mrs. Jefferson appeared from the kitchen and handed Will two sheets of paper set on top of eight or ten books. "I've noted the first sheet as authors with their addresses, phone numbers and e-mail addresses and this sheet lists the businesses he dealt with. This pile contains a copy of each author's latest effort." She began to cry a little. "I'm sorry" she said.

"That's all right." Will said. "We understand. You've been a big help. Now let us get out of here and get to work finding out who did this." He stood papers in hand, leaving Lou to carry the books. They both moved toward the foyer.

At the door Will turned to her and asked "There's one other small point Mrs. Jefferson, how was your husband's business doing? Was it running smoothly, profitable, that sort of thing?"

Wringing her hands, she looked directly into Will's kindly old eyes and the tears started in earnest and

Mrs. Jefferson blurted out, "Oh you're sure to find out soon enough. Business has been very bad. This economy has hurt a lot of small businesses and publishers are no different. They're dropping like flies right across the country. Those damned E-readers have devastated book sales. Authors won't wait for royalties and demand bigger advances. Printers want cash up front and book store owners, fighting the big box stores and the internet, are hurting like everyone else. They've become very difficult to deal with. They order smaller quantities and send them back for credit much faster than before. Everyone just passes their problem on to the guy at the bottom of the chain, the publisher. It has been tough these past few years."

She was distraught and scared but trying hard to be strong. Will stood watching her carefully, finally deciding she was being honest and that her veil of strength was rapidly shredding. He felt sorry for her.

"Have you friends to come and be with you? Is there anything we can do?" Will asked.

"Oh yes, our friends and relatives and the children, Leonard and his sister have been very good. I'll be fine but it's good of you to ask. Everyone has been wonderful and they've been beside me since he"…she took a deep breath and continued "you've both been very kind. Thank you" and she gently closed the door, tears running down both cheeks.

Chapter Six

Lou drove while Will studied the list of names and numbers Mrs. Jefferson printed for them. There were nine names in all, both male and female. None were familiar to Will because his reading tended toward pulp who-done-its' and the occasional smutty novel. Now, if Ian Stout was on the list, Will would have recognized it immediately, but alas, it was not. Mr. Jefferson's publishing empire hadn't reached that high.

Most on the list lived in the Hamilton, Burlington, Brantford area but there was one in Toronto, a couple with Mississauga addresses and another in Montreal. He liked the idea of interviewing the last author on the list and mentioned it to Lou.

"We'll have to work on Collin to finance a trip to Montreal. Crafty had an author named Kalishnikoff who lives there and I know for sure he has to be interviewed in person by both of us" he said with a sly grin.

"It would have to be an overnighter, eh" laughed Lou. "What did you say his name was, Kalishnikoff? What does he write about, machine guns?"

"Don't know, it doesn't say" Will said, missing the joke entirely "I guess we'll have to drive up, get a hotel and do the interview. After that we'll have dinner at one of those great Montreal bistros, of course with a bottle of wine or two. I know it will be tough but hell, someone's got to do it and it is our case so I'm sure Collin will understand."

"I'm sure" Lou agreed with a grin. This case was looking better already.

Will continued his scrutiny of the lists and made a note beside several names. He was surprised six of the nine authors were female and made a note of that.

The publisher's printer was in Quebec and Will made a note to get a map to see how far it was from Montreal. If not too great a distance, they might pay them a visit when they interviewed the Montreal author. That would strengthen their request for trip funding.

The balance of the drive back to the station was spent sorting out plans for visiting authors and contacting the companies with whom the victim had done business.

Will asked his partner to start a Google search of the names on their list. Lou loved computers and could sit for hours poking away at his keyboard, whereas Will barely tolerated them. They were a good mix, he, 'the old guy', using his ancient black dial phone sitting on his desk while Lou, the young good looking partner, did the electronic searches. Every couple of hours they'd get together to compare notes and findings, and make plans. Will wanted the search finished quickly so they could start interviewing the next morning.

As they pushed through the doors of the station Will let out a groan at the sight of the Spec's crime reporter bouncing out of a visitor's chair and making a beeline for them. "Hi guys, how ya doing?" he beamed.

It was Chad Williams, a five foot five impersonator of Jimmy Olsen of the Daily Planet wearing his best 'I'm a reporter' outfit. Most at the station considered him a pain in the ass.

Chad always wore jeans, polo shirt and a corduroy blazer. Not good corduroy, he was far too cheap for that. His was a genuine imitation corduroy jacket made in China. He always held a small open notepad in his left hand and had several pens and pencils jutting from his breast pocket to complete the image. The only thing he didn't have was a fedora sitting on the back of his head with a PRESS card stuck in the band. Will suspected Chad Williams watched a 'B' movie about reporters and police work every night when he went home.

"Not bad" muttered Lou and neither he nor Will stopped walking.

"Do you have any leads on who might have done in the book guy?" Chad said trying to keep up with them as they strode across the station lobby to the secure doors reporters couldn't go through.

"Nothing we can talk about" was all Will said.

"Awe come on guys. I need something to give my editor to get him off my back, eh." Chad slipped in a hint of whine at this point.

Will stopped and looked at the little twerp, thinking how he would be so happy getting away from this type of ruthless heartless garbage when he retired. He knew Chad was a lying bastard about getting hassled by his editor. This was Hamilton's first murder in eight months and Chad's superiors would be dancing around their offices in glee. Chad was just looking for something extra, hoping to score some brownie points. The old detective could hear the curly haired little jerk in the Press Club that night, crowing about his extraordinary investigative abilities.

He knew Chad Williams couldn't give a tinker's damn about the dearly departed if he couldn't score points by getting a tidbit ahead of anyone else. The reporter had all the attributes of a 'sleaze bag' news man and none of the good points. Hell, he couldn't even write worth a damn.

Taking a breath to help him control the impulse to tell the reporter to get stuffed, Will said carefully "Mr. Williams, we are in the early stages of our investigation of this heinous crime and I assure you and your readers that we will apprehend the person or persons who are responsible. With your vast experience in the world of crime reporting, you know how sensitive this early stage is. That is why we can say nothing at this time. If there is anything specific you may want, talk to Collin Fraser, the Chief of Detectives." Will smiled knowing it didn't look close to genuine, turned and pushed through the secure door leaving the reporter with nothing more than he had five minutes before their encounter.

"You handled that well, although Collin will kill you for that last bit" Lou said in admiration.

"Thank you. I hate the little bastard and would love to tell him to buzz off but Collin has told me at least a thousand times to be nice to the media. Let him handle the little twerp. How the hell anyone can be nice to a piece of camel crap like him is beyond me" he said, shaking his head.

Chapter Seven

Mrs. Jefferson's list was alphabetical and the top name was Drew, Rosanne Drew, so Will called to arrange an appointment. She was pleasant, almost jovial on the phone, and suggested in a cheery voice that he come around anytime he liked. Will asked if nine thirty the next morning would be alright and she happily agreed.

The next two were the same. Sonya Franks and Michael Kalishnikoff both seemed happy to welcome the police into their homes and answer any and all questions they might have. These people were all very cooperative and Will thought it was going just a wee bit too easy. He sensed dark clouds forming off in the distance, his years of experience telling him things weren't quite right. He was looking forward to the upcoming interviews.

Lou walked in just then and handed him a fist-full of papers and said, "Here are the print-outs of my search of our victim and his authors. It makes interesting reading" and stood quietly as Will shuffled through the pile.

"What are the important points?" the older man asked.

"Well, all have done one book and several have written two or more. There are a few good reviews but the matter of quality crops up more than a few times. One reviewer suggested the publisher find someone capable of spelling words with more than two letters to correct the author's mistakes in his next book. Another said he liked the book but it looked like it had been printed by a group of chimpanzees. He said the publisher should find a printer who owned a press made sometime in the twentieth century, preferably the latter part. Things like that." Lou reached across the desk and pointed to one paper.

"This Hamilton writer is the one suing the publisher in small claims and this one" he pointed to another page "is the Toronto author who has the eight hundred thousand dollar lawsuit in the works and there's another guy, Pommeroy, who has a suit against Jefferson as well."

"Pretty interesting" Will mused. "This will help us when we start the interviews, but if it wasn't a plain old smash and grab, we sure have a large question to answer. What was the motive? I doubt it was the guy suing for eight hundred large, what was his name? Yes, here it is, MacDonald, Duncan MacDonald. Hell he sounds like one of my own countrymen and we surly never kill an enemy before squeezing his last farthing from him. It's a time honored Highland tradition. You'd be daft to kill anyone until you have all his money." Will said as he smiled a mischievous grin at his partner.

"What the hell can you expect from barbarians who paint their faces blue and run around in skirts" laughed Lou.

"Kilts, ye daft twit, they be kilts" Will shot back, still grinning. "You see, that's how Scots took over the world. While your like were trying to figure out what we were wearing and constantly complaining about the bonny sound of our pipes, we Scots were canny enough to be building railroads, inventing telephones and steamboats and constructing the greatest ships in the world. Ye dinna even notice we were running everything" his Scottish brogue resonating around the room.

"OK, OK, I give up. If it wasn't for the Scots, we would all be speaking English" Lou shot back.

"Not bloody likely. You'd probably all be speaking German if it weren't for the brave lads who rushed in to save the English Kings and Queens so often." Will was on a good natured roll just as Collin Fraser stuck his head in the door.

"God, I should have known better than to put a square head and a pig headed Scot together as partners. You guys drive me crazy."

"Not to worry boss. My people know how to make good beer and his know how to make good whiskey. If we had gotten together in 1935 and compared notes there probably wouldn't have been a war. Anyway, we aren't shooting at each other, yet. What do you need?" Lou was grinning.

"I'm just checking on the Jefferson case, any headway?"

Will lost his accent to give Collin an update. "We talked to the widow who wasn't very merry, but then again, she wasn't all that unmerry either. We also have several interviews set for tomorrow. We will have to do an overnighter to Montreal later in the week to interview one author and visit the publisher's printers who are a few miles outside of the city. I'll get a requisition on your desk for that this afternoon" and he held his breath waiting for the argument.

Collin shrugged, looked from Will to Lou and back, then simply said "OK, I know it's a tough job but hey, someone has to do it. Just let me know and please, don't stay at the Chateau Champlain" and with a wink turned and left both of them standing with open mouths.

Chapter Eight

Rosanne Drew lived in the eastern section of Hamilton in a seventh floor apartment overlooking one of Kings Forest Golf Course's back nine holes. Situated at the back of the building with a large balcony above the fairway, her home was the perfect place for a writer.

Will rang her number on the call board in the foyer and she immediately buzzed them up.

Ms. Drew was not what they expected. Standing majestically awaiting them at the open door of her apartment, she was a sight to behold.

Long and lean and slightly over six feet tall, Rosanne Drew looked down on Will and straight into the eyes of Lou Shatz. Her age was hard to determine but Will figured it to be more than sixty and less than a hundred. Other than that, his guess was as good as anyone's.

Slender, actually thin, she was wearing a floor length dark blue skirt, loose white silk blouse and a short string of pearls around her long patrician neck. Her perfectly groomed white hair fell to the small of her back like a cascade of fresh snow. Looking every inch a lady in the old style, Rosanne Drew was the type of woman who caused people to turn and stare whenever she entered a room.

"How nice of you to be on time" she smiled as Will took her extended hand and stood for a moment, fighting an impulse to bend and kiss it. Instead he shook it gently and introduced himself and his partner.

"Sometimes it can be difficult" he said as she closed the door and ushered them into her sitting room.

"I understand Detective Deas, your duties must be very taxing and I'm sure you have many demands on your time. Please sit down and let me get you and your partner tea while you ask your questions."

"Please, don't go to any trouble for us."

"Oh it's no trouble. I come from a generation that considers making tea for a guest to be as natural as breathing. I know these days it's not necessary for one to be a good host or have manners, but I fail to fit into that category. Times have changed Detective Deas, but I haven't." Her smile was genuine if a little sad.

"That's very kind of you and we appreciate it."

Rosanne fussed with a small kettle and tea pot at the sideboard and asked over her shoulder "I assume you're here about the death of my publisher."

"Yes we are Ms. Drew, and I want to offer my condolences" Will answered.

"Oh goodness me, there's no need to do that" she laughed as she carried a silver tray with a flowered teapot and three exquisite teacups on saucers to the low table in front of them. Straightening up she looked at the two policemen and calmly spoke in words one would never expect from such a well-bred lady.

"Peter Jefferson was a rotten, no good sleazy little bastard and I can assure you the world is most definitely a better place without an asshole like him cluttering it up" Rosanne emphatically stated.

If she had lifted her skirt and peed on her expensive Afghan carpet right there in front of them, Will would not have been more surprised.

"I beg your pardon" he gasped.

"No need for that either. No pardon is necessary. Peter Jefferson was without question the most despicable man I have ever met, and believe me, I have met a lot of men during my many years and several of them were quite despicable. On a scale of one to a hundred that nasty little prick would probably rank somewhere around one hundred and seventy-five! No condolences or feigned remorse are needed! Now is a time to celebrate!" She smiled sweetly as she poured more tea.

Will looked at Lou and got a blank stare and a slight roll of the eyeballs.

"Your suggesting you're actually glad he's dead?" Will asked.

"Glad would be a gross understatement" she laughed. "I'm really deliriously happy, overjoyed, thrilled. I could sing like Julie Andrews and dance bare-footed on the grass of that golf course out there if the next foursome of golfers would allow it."

"Gentlemen, I'd be happy to contribute to the defense fund of the one who went to the trouble to rid the world of that piece of toxic garbage. Actually, you might want to call Greenpeace, or the Sierra Club or even those ninnies at PETA to see if they were the ones responsible. It would be the only thing of value any of them have done for this planet in the past ten years."

Will sat quietly looking at the face of this woman who at first seemed such a sweet aristocratic older lady. He thought he was correct in considering her a very impressive woman, but adjusted his assessment to include the phrase 'one tough old broad'.

"I must ask you a few questions about your dealings with the deceased and your movements over the past several days. Are you up to that?" Lou ventured to ask.

"Of course" she smiled, sipping lady-like with her little pinky extended from her teacup. "Ask away."

"How long have you dealt with Mr. Jefferson and Crafty Press?" Lou again.

"Seven horrid years" was her answer.

Not now surprised by this response he asked "Why horrid?"

"Well, the first six months weren't bad. I was excited at finally getting a publisher to take my book and the lying little twerp made all kinds of promises and treated me quite well. He even bought me lunch. I think he allocated enough money to buy one lunch per author, after that if you wanted to eat or drink - you paid." She poured more tea.

"Then what happened?" Will asked.

"As soon as he had my money the romance was over."

"What do you mean 'had your money', how did he get money from you?"

Rosanne Drew looked wistfully away from the two policemen for a moment before answering. Finally she said "the deal he offered to all his authors was basically the same. He would publish your book if you, the author, agreed by contract to purchase a large quantity of the books printed. It was a sweet deal for him and could be a good one for the author if things went well with the book."

"You've lost me" Will said, pen and notebook at the ready. "I think I'll need more detail. Could you explain this a little more, slowly?"

"It's quite simple if you have all the pertinent facts. First, he offers you a two thousand dollar advance on royalties to publish your book. This is the hook that brings you in. Then he says you must buy three hundred and fifty copies of the book at forty percent off list. That's the same rate as small bookstores and a little more than a big chain would pay. He sets the list price which is usually twenty dollars, so the author pays twelve dollars per copy. It means I give him a cheque for about forty-two hundred dollars plus tax and he hands me a two thousand dollar in advance royalties and an invoice for the books."

Will was making notes as was Lou. Both quickly saw how the system worked. He nodded to Rosanne to continue.

"You must realize it only costs about three dollars and fifty cents to print a book when you buy a thousand copies and the price goes down if you print more. In effect the author has handed him enough to pay for the advance plus the production of the first thousand books." She waited for them to stop scribbling before continuing.

"The thing is that most authors don't know about the grants" she continued.

"What grants?" Lou interrupted.

"Didn't you know? There's a plethora of fat provincial and federal grants to the arts sitting out there for those with knowledge or connections to get them. Actually they are welfare cheques dispensed by bored civil servants in response to applications filled with lies and deceptions. Those are the grants I'm talking about."

"You sound a little bitter?" Will said quietly.

"Used would be a better word. It's like being sweet talked into bed by some smooth fellow with promises of great wealth and lasting fame. When he's finished having his fun he treats you like dirt and you're left with the mess. Most women know what I mean." Again she smiled a sad smile.

"What amount of money would these grants be?" Lou persisted.

"If one works the system it would be somewhere between three and seven thousand per book. I've heard it averages about five thousand per."

Lou did more calculating in his book and looked at Will. "The Crafty website claims they produce eight to twelve books a year. That would represent forty to sixty thousands of income. Not bad when someone else pays for the books for which you get the grant."

Miss Drew gave them another tidbit of information at this point. "Remember as well, he has about six or seven hundred copies of your book that he can sell online or through bookstores across the country or in the United States. And he doesn't have to give you a penny because he's already given you an advance on the first thousand books, an advance you paid for. Any income from additional sales is all his.

"There are numerous places that will pay a dollar a book or place them on consignment at three to five dollars each. They can be remaindered in discount stores and he can pick up two or three dollars a copy. In a worst case scenario he can donate them to libraries and get a tax write off."

Lou looked from her to Will "This guy's publishing business could be very lucrative. With luck he could bring in a hundred grand a year."

"You're right, and with some creative accounting he would pay very little tax." Rosanne offered.

There was quiet in the small living room as the two policemen digested all they had heard. Although newly introduced to all the complexities of a business they had never encountered, these two experienced investigators knew a scam when one reared its ugly head.

"One would think the Government grant-giving agencies would control any untoward activities by a publisher" Lou suggested.

"Good Lord no" Ms. Drew laughed. "You forget, publishing is part of the sacrosanct world of the arts. If anyone dares question a member of the arts world they're called a Neanderthal or a 'knuckle dragging mouth breathing hillbilly' born and raised without culture. No Detective Deas, if Civil Servants suspect anything nefarious they simply start denying grants and hope the questionable person applying quietly fades from the picture."

Will thought about that for a moment then continued "Do you think all this type of manipulation would prompt someone to actually kill him?"

"Hell yes" she said quite forcefully. "I've thought of it myself several times but alas, someone beat me to it. And, for your information because I know you have to ask, I was in Windsor the night he was dispatched so very efficiently. I did a book signing that day at a large book store; stayed the night in a hotel and the next morning drove to another signing at a London book store on Oxford Street. I have the bills and the stores will confirm my attendance. I sold quite a few books in both stores."

"One last question" Will asked, "if he was such a rat, why would you keep doing business with his publishing company?"

"There was a contract. I knew nothing about publishing contracts and I made an incredible mistake right at the start by signing away my lifelong writings to him and his company. If I went anywhere else with my work before offering it to him, he could stop me. If another publisher wanted to publish one of my books he would have to pay Crafty Press or face an injunction or a lawsuit. Publishers, like most businessmen, are cowards when it comes to lawsuits so none would touch me while under contract to Crafty. I had no choice." Rosanne Drew was a bitter tough old lady.

Will and Lou exchanged glances knowing they had enough from this interview. They closed their books in unison and stood, Will taking out his card.

"I want to thank you for your help Ms. Drew. We may have to talk to you again so here is my card. If you have to leave town for an extended time, please call and let me know your schedule."

Within minutes they were walking down the hall to the elevators knowing the now happy, but still bitter old lady was standing in her doorway watching them.

Chapter Nine

Sonya Franks was next and her background was quite different from their first interviewee.

She was the daughter of a bad tempered heavy drinking foundry worker who hurt his wife and children, so at seventeen, to get out of the house and away from him, Sonya got pregnant and married her steel worker lover. Her husband was a dreamer who over the next several years searched for ways of making it big while helping her make five babies.

This dreamer was not afraid of hard work and saved everything he earned from a part time second job at an all-night gas station. Finally, with these savings and what he could scrape together from family and friends, he bought a Tim Horton's donut franchise before they were worth a fortune. His wife thought him nuts but stood by him while most of his friends were offended by his efforts to be anything other than a steel worker. It didn't matter, he wanted more than that.

Sonya Franks and her husband worked side by side during the lean years before Tim Horton's coffee and donuts became a Canadian addiction, but, when they did, Sonya and her man reaped the benefits.

They now lived in the best section of the east mountain and had in their backyard the only in-ground pool in either family. Their children went to the best private schools and universities with one gaining admission to Harvard Law School. Mr. Frank's decision to give up the foundry floor for the donut kitchen seemed like a pretty good one.

Sonya was waiting for them that morning, sitting contentedly on the front porch of her home on their quiet tree lined street.

Whereas the first lady they interviewed was tall and sophisticated, Mrs. Franks was short, a little plump, and motherly. Will liked her immediately and could easily imagine her in a kitchen wearing a flour covered apron slipping a pie into the oven.

She was in her fifties, with a nice tan and wearing some very expensive jewelry on both hands. She also had the clothes sense of a high class Paris designer and it was obvious she had the means to shop where she wanted, regardless of price.

"Hello gentlemen" she said with a smile "please come in" and guided them into her home.

It was an elegant place, indicative more of classy rather than ostentatious spending. Several of the carpets and furniture pieces were antiques but all blended together to create an atmosphere of quiet, genteel upper class living. The house reeked of good taste, thoughtful purchases and style. It was like one of the great homes in Scotland and Will loved it.

This time it wasn't tea but coffee from a pot into mugs sitting on a unique glass table held up by two ceramic elephant feet. Will had never seen one quite like it.

They accepted the coffee and went through the preliminary steps and once done, moved ahead with their first question.

"As you already know we are here because of the untimely death of your publisher, Mr. Peter Jefferson. Could you describe to us your relationship with him?"

"Certainly," recalled Mrs. Franks. "Five years ago, after two years of rejections by more than fifty publishers and agents in both Canada and the United States, I received a letter from Crafty Press indicating an interest in my story summary. The letter asked for a copy of the complete manuscript. I was elated, excited and actually danced about this room waving the letter above my head."

"How did he know about your book?" Lou asked.

"I had sent him a submission. It's what authors do when trying to get published. You see, writing the story is often the easiest part. Getting someone to even read it, and then have then actually publish it, can be the biggest hurdle to get over and can often take years." She poured more coffee and continued.

"Once you finish your story you make up what is called a query letter plus a biography and a brief one page summary of the complete story. You stick all that and the first three chapters into an envelope and you send it to ten or twenty different publishers. After that you wait and wait and wait. Believe me, some of the publishers never acknowledge your submission but many do and after eighteen or nineteen rejections, any positive response from a publisher, any publisher, is reason to celebrate."

"I delivered my manuscript to Mr. Jefferson's home that day and five days later he contacted me and invited me to his place to discuss my story and the possibility that he might publish it. I was in heaven. I went, entered into contract negotiations and we finalized a deal within a couple of weeks."

Lou interjected "did the deal involve you giving Crafty Press any money?"

"Yes, how did you know? Peter explained that if an author had faith in their work, he or she should take some risk themselves and not expect a publisher to take it all. The way he laid it out seemed to make sense. He explained how I would get all my money back and a lot more from sales resulting from the tremendous effort and expense Crafty Press would put into marketing. It was a great sounding package." Sonya spread her hands and smiled the sad smile of someone who knew they'd been conned.

"What happened next Mrs. Franks?" Will prodded.

"Within days of the launch I realized the only tremendous effort I'd ever see from Peter Jefferson and Crafty Press was the effort to get my check! With that done, any marketing, promotion or selling of my book by them faded into the mist. I was left on my own. When I asked why my book wasn't in certain bookstores he would blame it on his incompetent distributor and suggest I go into each store and arrange for them to handle my work.

"When I asked him who his distributor was, the lying little twerp told me he had just fired the last one because he was lazy and stupid and Crafty was in the process of getting a new one. I don't know if he ever had a distributor that he fired or if he ever got a new one. The problem was always someone or something else but never him. I soon learned not to expect anything from him" again the wringing of the hands and the sad smile.

"Why have you stayed with him?" Will asked.

"I signed a damned contract that contained the phrase 'this book and all other books by author Sonya Franks'. That means everything I ever write must go to him first. He then has six months to evaluate it and if he wants it, the same conditions apply as they did with the first book. If he doesn't want it, I can do as I please with it. Of course he always wants the book, so I'm stuck."

"Is there any way you can get out of the contract?" Lou asked.

"Sure, he told me exactly how to get out when I asked him a couple of years ago. He said bring a certified check for fifty thousand and he would give me an unconditional release. I said thank you and hung up."

Will had the next question.

"Where were you on the evening he died?"

"Here, with my husband. We had a late supper because my husband had a meeting with his managers and he came home about seven. We then took an hour after our meal to finish a nice bottle of Beaujolais and went to bed just after the eleven o'clock news."

"How did you hear about the death of Mr. Jefferson?" Lou asked.

"Jennifer North, she's another author in the same bind as me. She was in Calgary visiting friends and called me when the story broke. She told me to turn on the news and open the champagne." Sonya smiled a guilty but happy smile.

"You're pleased about this turn of events, are you?" Will said.

"Of course I am. Elated would be a better word. He was a rotten bastard who won't be missed by anyone other than those to whom he owes money. He was a sleaze bag. Ask any of the women he had contracted to Crafty Press. Ask them if they ever felt his hand on their backside or brushing across their breast." She stared darkly at them.

"I remember one book launch where the little piece of scum took a run at the new author's wife right out in front of his own wife. Everyone in the room saw it except the new author who was busy signing books. The new author's wife handled it with class and got away from the slime ball before her husband found out because I think 'Peter the Pig' would have gotten a boot up his backside." She stopped and waved her hand across her face as though shooing a bad memory away, the way one might shoo a fly.

"I didn't kill him but I sure thought of it a few times." Sonya Franks said firmly. "Peter Jefferson was a man with only one good deed in this world to his credit. He was able to find a nasty person in an alley and managed to provoke him into committing murder. For that single deed his killer has earned the gratitude of a lot of people."

Chapter Ten

Will and Lou stopped for lunch at a small diner on Concession Street to try and digest both some food, and the revelations from their visits with Rosanne Drew and Sonya Franks. They needed a little time comparing notes and first impressions, knowing one might see or hear something the other had missed.

"What do you think?" Will asked between mouthfuls of beef barley soup.

"I'm not quite sure what to think" Lou shrugged. "I've never seen so many happy people in a murder investigation in all my time on the force. Hell, I'm willing to bet ten bucks the hanging of Saddam Hussein had fewer smiling faces."

"I know, and I have a feeling none of the other authors will be any different."

Lou pulled his notebook from his jacket and flipped it open. "You're right" he grinned. "That last one, Sonya, used just about every derogatory adjective in the book to describe her publisher. I wrote some of them down. Things like pig, bastard, twerp, sleazy and scum and we must remember she was in a good mood because he was dead. I'd hate to hear what she called him if she was in a bad mood with him alive."

"I noticed that too" slurped Will. "The first author, Drew, was the same. She had some blistering descriptive phrases of him as well. From the looks of it, our Mr. Jefferson had a bad reputation, at least with women. I wonder if his male writers felt the same. It will be interesting to see if they were lining up to see him dead as well. His wife is the only one we've met who didn't rip him apart."

Lou turned back a page, remembering something. "The credit reports came in this morning from Equifax and Tran-Canada and I glanced at them before you got in. He owed just about everyone in town and some of it goes back quite a way. He has several judgments and an order or two against him. He's been in and out of small claims court enough to qualify for an honorary law degree. The reports paint a sad picture."

"Everything is in his wife's name, I'd suppose" said Will.

"You got it. He's pretty slick, although there are a couple of names in the reports that would cause me concern if I owed them money. Especially if I didn't pay up when asked." Lou spun his notes around and pointed to the name of a construction company run by some very rough people.

"Interesting, he actually owed money to their company?"

"Yep" Lou said. "I don't know how much or if it was paid but I was surprised to see it on the Equifax list. Can you imagine those thugs reporting one of their loans to a local credit bureau? I know they try to appear legitimate but this is ridiculous."

"Tax laws" Will said with an unhappy grin. "They do some honest work and one of their accountants suggests they list it as corporate business and if there's a default, there's a tax loss. Besides, Jefferson was an old newspaper man and they probably hit him hard on interest but they wouldn't do anything illegal, he knew too many people who could write a story about loan sharking."

Lou shook his head and finished his coffee. He was a newcomer with just under five years on the force, none walking a beat and only a year into his gold shield. He had cut his teeth patrolling Hamilton's streets in a car, a cocoon really, up in the safe quiet East Mountain region.

Lou was sharp and very smart but before he could be called a well-rounded cop he needed a lot more street education on the difference between who the bad people were, and who were just stupid or misguided.

Will considered himself fortunate in the street smarts department, getting his pavement education beside an old man considered by many the best beat cop on the force. That canny old man knew every hooker, drug addict, fence, drunk and thief in the city. He also knew the sad cases, the lonely ones without the mental ability to operate in their complex world. He taught his young partner the difference.

Will learned who all the inhabitants of Railway Street were on a first name basis as well as much of the details of their vending machine business. He was well aware of the Duke's Lounge in the old Royal Connaught Hotel where large men in dark blazers and black turtle neck sweaters sat quietly guarding other men, most with last names ending in a vowel.

He knew when the Don from the Buffalo mob family was in town and where he was, usually the Duke's Lounge, and with whom he was chatting. Will's education with old Pat Ryan on the gritty streets of industrial Hamilton ran a lot deeper than what most young officers received.

"Well Lou, this killing is getting more interesting by the minute and the more we know the easier it's going to be to clear up. We can't see Mrs. Henning for a couple of days because she's on her way back from Egypt and the writer in Brantford is tied up today so why don't we go back to the station, sort out what we've done up to now and make arrangements to drive up to Montreal tomorrow" and he dropped a few loonies on the table and made for the door.

Chapter Eleven

The obituary of Peter James Jefferson appeared in the Hamilton Spectator two days after his death and was picked up by several papers across Canada. As word of the killing of this obscure publisher, and the odd way he had been done in spread through the literary landscape, a mild interest began to build. Quill and Quire, the bible of the publishing industry had a brief and very neutral comment in its 'News of the Industry' section, making everyone who was anyone in the Canadian book world aware of the event.

Peter Jefferson was known by many but in most cases only by reputation. At an upscale Toronto book signing held the evening the comment appeared in Quill and Quire, one publishing executive mentioned the murder of Jefferson to another and the answer he got was, 'who?'

When the first executive explained it was the heavy drinking long haired guy from Hamilton who ran a subsidy house, his colleague remembered.

"Oh I know who you mean. I met him once at the Frankfort Book Fair several years ago. If I remember correctly he was an obnoxious little jerk. Someone killed him, eh? Too bad" and he changed the subject to a new line of cookbooks the questioner was producing. It was a common response.

Since it was a slow news cycle and because the victim was a publisher murdered with his own pen, the Toronto press corps took more than a passing interest in the story. Each outlet assigned a junior to look into the story and because many rode bicycles or just hated traffic, they took to the phones to get copy. After all, Hamilton was forty-five miles away, a place most Toronto people considered to far a distance to travel without getting on a plane.

Within hours Collin Fraser was forced to designate a special line for the case and assign a civilian member of staff to handle the calls. He also left a note for Will to get the bloody case solved so he could have some peace.

Along with this media activity were random calls from the general public offering a wealth of information about the deceased's activities and lifestyle. This was all funneled through the station and onto Will's desk with copies to Lou. When all the tips were combined they painted a grotesque picture of a person one couldn't call a very nice man.

The majority of the stories were about his drinking. He was a regular in the Dundas bar where he was on the night he was murdered. He was also well known in several other watering holes, including Hamilton's Press Club situated near Hamilton's City Hall. People in all his haunts knew him to stagger out to his car, fumble with his keys and roar off. On several occasions attempts were made to get his keys or call a cab but Peter Jefferson was a mean drunk. He would curse, swear and threaten to bash anyone who interfered. The regulars and staff at all these places quickly learned to keep away.

There were as many calls about his almost non-stop womanizing. Mr. Jefferson fancied himself as one of God's gifts to the weaker sex and spread his favors about with wild abandon, limiting his hanky panky only to those hours he was awake and sober enough to perform.

Several calls referred to motels around the city that he frequented with various ladies and a couple of calls were from females who alleged they were forced to do things they normally didn't do.

One anonymous call was from a husband who suggested the whore-mongering son-of-a-bitch was well done dead and the police should start checking every married man in town if they wanted suspects.

As Will and Lou built a profile of the victim they discovered a smiling suspect under every rock they looked under.

The dead man was the target of so much dislike that both were now convinced the crime was not a random accidental killing by an incompetent thief. They were sure someone wanted Jefferson dead and figured out how to do it. Both detectives had their own idea on who did the deed but kept it close to their chest. They thought they'd narrow it down after they had talked to all the authors and investigated his personal life a little more.

There was also the matter of the victim's dealings with a very tough group of people who made loans and were known to break arms and legs when the money wasn't paid as agreed! Occasionally these businessmen were suspected of calling in outside help to kill a badly delinquent borrower as a means of setting an example. This had to be followed up.

In most murder investigations the problem was figuring out who may have wanted the victim dead. That sure as hell wasn't the trouble here. They had suspects enough to populate a small town, a very happy small town full of laughing people dancing and singing in the streets with glasses of wine in their hands.

Chapter Twelve

Lou and Will left early the next morning for their six hour trip to Montreal and their interview with Michael Kalishnikoff, author of several highly respected cookbooks.

The drive through the eastern Ontario countryside was relaxed and pleasant once they were out of the Greater Toronto area and they included a short stop for an early lunch in Kingston.

It was sunny and warm with a light breeze near the waterfront of the old city and they would have sat all day sipping beers in the sidewalk café had there not been work to do. With some reluctance they got back on the road and headed for the Quebec border.

Will had spent a lot of time in Montreal over the years and always looked forward to another visit. It had a vibrancy and life not found in most cities where the main reason for existence was making a dollar. The citizens of Montreal were more interested in getting out of the office to relax in a bar or café or just sitting outside in the sun watching the world pass by. As one moved away from Ontario's heartland and closer to old Montreal, the atmosphere of a city with more on its mind than money became apparent.

Michael Kalishnikoff's small flat was perched above a bakery on a narrow side street in what was called Old Montreal. As the two detectives drove into the area they felt they had somehow left the Western

Hemisphere and motored into a city in Europe, untouched by time. It was clear the do-gooders who led the Urban Renewal campaigns in other Canadian cities during the fifties and sixties made little headway in Montreal.

These government sponsored busy-bodies had arrived on the scene with truckloads of taxpayer's money declaring late nineteenth and early twentieth century housing obsolete and in need of replacement, like worn out shoes. They went about wrecking whole neighborhoods, replacing sturdy inexpensive homes with characterless rows of new townhouses or butt-ugly 'project' high rise buildings. Fortunately for everyone it didn't happen in Montreal.

The tiny parks popping haphazardly into Will's view as they drove the narrow streets would have been eliminated and replaced by wide expanses of grass you wouldn't be allowed to walk on. Parking, instead of being a blood sport as it was now, would be regulated to a paved spot set in a far corner of the new complex with designated places for each tenant. Visitors would have to apply to the management office for a temporary parking pass. The people of Montreal were spared these horrors and now lived in one of the most interesting and beautiful cities in North America. Having visited many times Will loved Montreal, but it was Lou's first encounter and by the time they found the author's street he was totally captivated.

After finding a parking space the old Scot and his trusty sidekick climbed the outside iron stairs beside the sweet smelling bakery and knocked on the only door at the top. It opened immediately.

"Welcome my friends, welcome. Please come in and make yourselves comfortable." This was not what they had expected.

Michael Kalishnikoff was over eighty and looked sixty, maybe sixty-five in bad light. He was about five feet eight, just a little over two hundred pounds and sported a beautifully trimmed white beard that made him look a bit like the Santa Claus in 'Miracle on Forty Second Street', only better groomed.

Sounding like the master of Downton Abbey, he asked "Do tell me, are you coffee or tea drinkers? I know it's a little early for anything stronger but I have that too, if you like."

"Goodness no" Will laughed. "Coffee's fine but please don't go to any bother."

"No bother, none at all," Michael said cheerily. "Please, make yourselves comfortable and I'll fix us a pot. It'll take but a minute" and he hurried into his tiny kitchen.

Within minutes the author was sitting in an armchair across from them, smiling and apparently ready, willing and able to assist them in their search for their murderer.

"Now gentlemen, you have come a long way at great expense to your taxpayers to pry from my head some tidbits to aid you in your investigation, so pry away, what can I do for you?"

"Well sir, we can start by going over your history of dealings with Mr. Peter Jefferson and his company Crafty Press," Will Said.

"No problem, fire away."

"Good. First off, how long have you been associated with Mr. Jefferson and his company?"

"About six years."

"And how has that relationship been?"

"Quite ghastly!" Michael said, still smiling.

"How was it ghastly?" Will felt he was beginning to talk like the old fellow opposite.

"Well, I would have to say it had been rather ghastly because one never knew what was going to happen next. Your victim Jefferson, in discussing a business matter, would state one thing on Monday and on the following Wednesday would claim he never said such a thing. He'd insist something completely different had been said and then berate you for making things up as though you were the liar, not him. I then started making notes during our telephone conversations but finally gave up. From that point on I demanded all communication be in writing."

"You mean he would tell you a lie?" Lou chipped in.

"Tell me a lie? My good man, he always lied. When his lips were moving he was lying. I think I'm safe in using Mary McCarthy's famous line about Lillian Hellman and apply it to my publisher by saying 'every word he spoke was a lie, including 'and' and 'the'. She could have well been speaking of the unloved and finally departed Mr. Peter Jefferson."

There was no doubt in either of his guest's minds regarding the author's low opinion of the publisher.

"You sound much like other authors we've interviewed. None of them seemed very sorry about Mr. Jefferson's demise" said Will.

"Very sorry? Goodness me, not at all. I would think they are all deliriously happy, ecstatic. I can see them dancing about with drinks in their hands, singing cheery ditties and toasting the one who removed such a person from our planet. Even I opened a bottle of champagne to celebrate, not my best of course, but an adequate one just the same. No, my good members of the police force, few writers are such hypocrites that they would feign sadness or remorse over the passing of Peter the Piss Poor Publisher, as one of my colleagues always called him."

"That would be Ms. Drew I think. I believe she referred to him with those words." Lou interjected.

"Oh yes, dear sweet Rosanne. He treated her so badly and she just let the little bastard walk all over her. If he had done the same to me I might well have stuck a pen into him myself." Michael was now quite stern at the mention of Rosanne Drew.

"We didn't say how he died sir, how did you know?" Will asked.

"Good Lord man, everyone knows. Rosanne called me the morning following the wonderful evening he was struck down and gave me all the delightful details. It was in the local papers and I saw it on CBC news last night. Even Quill and Quire mentioned it. My goodness it's such a juicy story and the way he died makes it all the more fun. Imagine a publisher being killed with a fountain pen! Poetic justice I would call it. Hell, I doubt if Raymond Chandler could have written a better scene."

The three men silently sipped their coffees for several moments before Will continued "could you tell us what you were doing the night Mr. Jefferson was murdered?"

The author leaned back in his chair and laughed.

"Of course I can. In fact I'm quite flattered you think I could do such a service for mankind. It's a rather nice compliment. Thank you. I'm eighty-one years old you know and although I seem chipper and able to flit about this place with little trouble, my staying power is gone and I must rest much more often than I ever did."

"As for getting from Montreal to Hamilton you can check the airlines, the bus companies and VIA rail to assure yourself I didn't avail myself of their services. You'll find I didn't."

"Now you may say I could quietly take my car and drive there and back. That is a possibility but although my car is not quite as old as me, it is old enough to legally drink alcohol in this province. I doubt it would do the thousand mile return trip even if I promised it premium gas" he said with a grin.

"But you haven't told us what you were doing that night" Will persisted.

"Oh yes, you're right, I haven't, have I? Well gentlemen, while your unknown villain was sticking a pen into Peter's skin, I sat in a delightful little restaurant not far from here called Sans Menu, that means 'without a menu' in French. It's a wonderful little place where they write a new menu on a chalk board every day and bring it to your table. They only serve in the evening what was fresh on the market that morning. It could be fish, lamb, pork, whatever, but you can be sure it is fresh. Let me get you their card, you should try it tonight if you can. You'll love it" and he went to a small desk, pulled open a drawer and rummaged around in it.

"Oh, here's their card. Try them, they're on Rue Notre Dame West and they'll verify my presence for the evening in question. And here's another card. This is Carlo Makassian's card. He's a TV and movie actor, actually a very good one who lives in Guelph, in your area. He was up here for an audition. I let him sleep on the sofa and took him to dinner at Sans Menu. It saves him the price of a hotel and I enjoy his company. He arrived early evening, we went for a great meal including two bottles of Saint-Emilion, and he stayed the night. Carlo left about eight the next morning for his audition and then headed home. Call him, he'll verify all this." Michael handed the two cards to Will and refilled their coffee cups.

Will sat quietly looking across at their host, thinking about the things he had just heard. Michael was obviously not the person who went about killing publishers. Will knew instinctively the details of the cookbook writer's activities would check out and he also knew this sophisticated and articulate man could give him more insight into the victim's character. Will decided to change tact.

"Mr. Kalishnikoff, my partner and I have heard a litany of complaints about Mr. Jefferson but I'm having trouble pinning down what drove him to be the way he was. Can you give us some insight into his character, his motivations….what made him the way he was?"

The elderly author sat for some time thinking about his answer. With elbows on the arms of his chair he set the fingertips of his left hand on the fingertips of his right and placing his thumbs on his chin he gently touched the tip of his nose with his forefingers. Eyes flicking from one detective to the other, Michael the cookbook writer finally took a deep breath, dropped his hands and spoke.

"I believe Peter had an almost pathological need to prove he was as smart and as capable as anyone else in the world. He was like Fredo in the Godfather, believing he was smart when no one else really agreed."

"Peter was quite a short fellow and short men certainly have been known to be driven to prove something. History is littered with men who were very short and out to prove something.

"Churchill was only five six, Napoleon the same as was Martin Luther King Jr. Did you know Gandhi was five foot three, Beethoven the same and Lenin was five foot five. Hell, Stalin, Hitler and that bastard Khrushchev were all runts as well. Over the years short people have had a habit of being a pain in the ass. That's what your victim was, a pain in the ass.

"He always had to win, even when his win was meaningless. It was the winning that counted because if he won it meant you lost and it was very important to him to beat you. Along with needing to win was his terrible habit of gloating. You know, making sure you knew he won and you lost. It was pathetic to see his glee when he won some insignificant point."

"He was jealous of anyone who seemed more popular than him, who was better liked or better looking. When he ran into someone like that, he would set about besting them in any way he could." Michael took a sip of his now tepid coffee. Leaning back he thought for a moment and then continued.

"As an example, Peter wrote a couple of books himself and had a formal launch for each one. Getting people out to a launch is like pulling teeth and an unknown author is lucky if he can muster up twenty-five to thirty people, including relatives, because they all know they'll be expected to buy a copy and stand in line to get it signed."

"I remember he signed a new author several years ago who had arranged his own book launch which was fine with Peter because it meant he didn't have to pay for the launch. He insisted he would be the Master of Ceremonies and after some hesitation the author agreed. When Peter walked into the banquet room where the launch was held he found a hundred and fifty people with wine glasses clutched in their hot little hands. He was stunned. This was unheard of for a new writer and although Peter did a splendid job as MC, he hated the party and even more, the writer. Over the next few years he made that author's life miserable and never let up." Michael sighed, sitting back into his chair.

"I know you need to know what kind of man Peter Jefferson was and I hope you realize he was far too complex a human being to sum up in one or two sentences. He was devious, conniving, rude and dishonest. If I had to describe him with one word I'd have to say he was a shit."

Will finished scribbling notes and set his pen down.

"Can you think of anyone who hated him enough to kill him?"

"Yes, I could come up with a list but you have neither the time nor the paper and unless you have a dozen extra pens, you also don't have the ink to write out that list. Just start it with my name, put Rosanne Drew as number two and then jot down' the rest of humanity'. I told you, he was a shit." There was no humor in Michael's comments.

"Do you have any trips or a vacation planned for the next month or so?" Lou asked.

"Not at all, I'm working on my new cookbook. Leave me your card and I'll send you a copy, its Russian cooking, you'll love it. Now I must find a new publisher and that will take me some time. Life's tough but I think I'll survive." The author smiled.

"Good. We may have a few more questions for you but I think we'll be able to do them by phone or e-mail." Lou closed his notebook and looked at Will.

"Time to go I think" Will said and stood. "You've been most helpful Mr. Kalishnikoff, we appreciate your candor and insight" and he stuck out his hand.

"It is my pleasure Detective Deas" he said, warmly shaking the offered hand before guiding them to the door.

"Although it's a shame when someone dies prematurely, the shame varies from death to death. A child's death is by far the greatest shame for their potential is snuffed out. An artist's death, such as a painter, singer or writer, is a shame as well because we lose what they were offering. A close friend or relative's death is a shame also, because part of us dies with them and their passing leaves a hole in our lives. None of these apply to the death of Peter Jefferson. The only real shame about his death is that it didn't happen sooner" the still smiling writer said as he closed the door.

Chapter Thirteen

Three men sat in a corner of the public bar of the Empire Hotel, nestled at the intersection of Hughson and James Streets in Hamilton's oldest section. This was an area the local tourist promoters would never suggest you visit and if a tour bus was driving you through it to the waterfront, they'd turned up the canned music and stepped a little harder on the gas.

The Empire was a throwback to the days when city hotels were not where you slept but where you went to drink. In those days Ontario's Blue Laws forbade alcohol consumption anywhere except where you lived or in a licensed hotel where people did live. Hotels were soon devoting far more space to drinking rooms than to sleeping rooms. The laws also said you had to be seated to have a drink, and you could only have one drink per person at your table. There was no law saying you couldn't smile while drinking, but few did because the beer parlors, as they were called, were not inviting and certainly not pretty. They were just functional.

As the years passed, drinking became an acceptable activity in Ontario and the Blue Laws changed, but many of the neighborhood hotels hadn't. The Empire was one of them and stubbornly maintained its dour décor and grumpy looking male clientele.

The largest of the three men, known around the city as 'Tough Tony' stopped stuffing forkfuls of French fries into his mouth and asked "Who do you think did it?"

"I don't know but the boss is out seven large and he is not a happy man" Al, the gray haired, shorter and least robust of the trio said. "If it turns out he was whacked by someone we know, look out, 'cause they'll pay dearly." He waved his empty beer bottle impatiently at the waiter.

The three men, all employees of Fredrick Trapani or Freddie the Fox, reputed Godfather of Hamilton and southern Ontario, were discussing the murder of Peter Jefferson and the money he owed their boss.

The quiet one, Dominic, younger and better looking than Tony or Al, and wearing a much more expensive suit and black turtleneck shirt, set his coffee mug down. He had the air of one in charge and both of his companions shut up when he spoke.

"I'm sure it wasn't someone we know. I'd say it was a rank amateur. You wait. The cops will track him down and he'll be some dumb-ass dope head who made a mistake while collecting for his next hit."

"Ya think?" asked Tony.

"Sure. First off why would you rob someone at the back door of a bar just as the bar was closing? The papers say it happened after one o'clock, just when waiters and cooks are heading home. Do you think a pro would risk having some bimbo waitress stumble into him while he rifled through the stiff's pockets?

Hell he'd have to kill her too. No, the time was wrong and the place was wrong." Dominic took a sip of his coffee while the other two waited.

"Someone who knew what he was doing would have waited over near his car or even broke into it and waited in the back seat. Why hit him in the open, a good fifty feet from the shadows? No, I think it was done by a guy as stupid or wasted as the dead guy."

"You may be right Dom, you make sense, as usual" laughed Tony.

"Whatever, we have to see if we can find out who did it. Freddie won't be fit to live with if we don't" Dom said.

"Hell he's hardly fit to live with at the best of times" Al muttered. "This ain't no different." They all laughed at that.

"OK" Dom directed. "Tony, you have a few connections at the cop shop. See what you can find out. That broad in records should be able to help, you know, Shelly. Get on to her and see what you can find out."

"Man would I ever like to get 'on to her'. That's been a dream of mine for quite a few years" the big man grinned.

"You know what I mean" was all Dom said.

"Al, see what you can find out from your friends at the Spec. You know, that little asshole reporter who does the crime beat, the one who we're always slipping Leaf and Jay's tickets to. It's time he pays back and gives us what he has. Lean on him and see what you can find out."

"OK" was all Al said.

"Good, if you come up with anything call me. Otherwise we'll meet here tomorrow for lunch, and I'll buy. OK?"

Neither of Dominic's companions answered. They knew an order when one was given and both would be in the same seats for lunch the next day. Right now it was time to finish their drinks and get working.

Chapter Fourteen

Peter Jefferson's funeral was set for the Thursday of the week after his death.

The coroner's office had finally worked its way through all the tests and checks they could think of to delay releasing the body, and many people, including most of the media, were beginning to ask when the ceremony would take place.

The obit in the Spectator was small. The widow considered it a waste of her limited funds to place a large obituary deep in the bowels of the local daily. She knew the paper would splash the release of the body and the plans for the funeral across the front page, including details of her husband's life, so she figured why bother duplicating it. In a way it was the final insult to a man who lived all his life in the literary world. An obituary of less than seventy-five words with no mention of his business, career, or the books he'd written.

The Funeral home on King Street was in the heart of Dundas, less than a mile from the bar where Peter was murdered. Parking was not adequate for the crowd expected, but again the widow insisted her fiscal position kept her from paying for additional police to control traffic. She simply said she couldn't afford it and people would just have to make do. The funeral director was appalled but had the grace not to push the issue. Mrs. Jefferson also wanted a closed casket, with cremation to follow. It would be cheaper and she wouldn't have to purchase a cemetery plot.

On the morning of the funeral, a television satellite truck plunked itself in a no parking zone directly across the street from the funeral home. The crew leisurely placed red safety cones on every flat spot they could find and started setting up two stationary cameras. One was wrestled onto the roof of the van while the other placed near the front bumper. It was to capture reports breathlessly presented by a blonde beauty who at the moment was primping and vogueing for her adoring fans at the rear of the unit.

Within minutes, two CBC news vans arrived, one piloted by French staff, the other containing an English language trio. They pulled up in front of and behind the larger first unit with the camera on its roof and proceeded to place their red cones everywhere.

Will and Lou watched all this from an unmarked car sitting on the parking lot of an automotive repair plaza across and just up from the funeral home. Will passed his binoculars to his partner and pointed toward the blonde who had one high heeled foot on the rear bumper of the truck, slowly smoothing and straightening her panty hose, apparently oblivious to the three young Frenchmen staring wide eyed through the window of their van just ten feet behind her.

"This has all the earmarks of a full-fledged media circus" Will said.

"Or a porn show" Lou grinned. "She certainly has nice legs though."

The two policemen watched as more members of the media arrived and started preparations to hassle any non-media mourners attending. Cameras were tested for the mandatory close up of the grieving widow's tears and recorder batteries checked to ensure not one sob or wail of anguish was missed during the service. All appeared in order and soon the men had circled the leggy blonde while the other females in the press scrum gathered fifteen feet away to shoot nasty looks in her direction.

"Looks like show time in a few minutes" Lou said as he scanned the growing crowd of media. "I think Mrs. Jefferson just arrived, here, take a look" and he handed the glasses back to Will.

"It's her and the two kids. God, they're a scruffy pair. They look like Goths going to a funeral" and laughed quite heartily at his unintended joke. "I can't believe I said that" Will muttered between giggles while giving the binoculars back to Lou.

Lou looked bleakly at his partner and just shook his head "You Scots are a hard bunch" was his only comment.

As Will opened his door Lou reached over touching his arm and pointing. "Take a look. Isn't that big guy in the black shirt and black suit Tough Tony?"

"It sure as hell isn't the undertaker. Maybe he's here to make sure Jefferson is dead. You know, seeing that the whole thing isn't a fake just to get out of paying. I've heard of them sticking pins into stiffs just to be sure" and he grinned at Lou.

"Like I said, you Scots are a hard bunch."

As they strolled across the street toward the gathering, Will noted how few actual mourners had arrived during the past half hour. An elderly couple entered just behind the widow and her children and a few other assorted non-media types had straggled in during the set up. Will figured the ratio at about five to one - five from the press looking for a story to one paying respects to the dearly departed. As they approached the epicenter of it all he heard the blonde beauty's director count her down to start her spiel.

"This is Brenda Cornwallis live in Dundas at the funeral home where services are about to begin for well-known local publisher Peter Jefferson who was brutally murdered seven days ago in a parking lot not far from here" she paused a moment for effect and to get the correct look of sadness on her face before continuing.

"Mourners have been pouring in for the past half hour to pay their respects to this well-loved member of the literati both here in Canada and around the world. Mr. Jefferson was struck down in what police say was a 'botched robbery' that turned violent as he approached his car after an evening at a well-known local restaurant. The investigations are continuing."

Will and Lou hung back from the group fearing they would be spotted and called on to make a comment. They need not have worried as all eyes were on the lady holding the microphone.

The blonde continued "We're going in now for the service and we'll get back to you later with some statements from the many mourners. Back to you in the studio, Stan" and she ended her bit with a flourish and a dazzling smile at the camera. Will expected applause to erupt from the surrounding group of panting males.

It was then he saw Chad Collins from the Spectator pull in behind the CBC van in his soon to be condemned pick-up truck. Will grabbed Lou's arm and shoved him toward the open funeral home doors whispering "Let's get in before that asshole spots us."

The service was short and rather bland. It was obvious the funeral home's default rector knew his clichés far better than he knew the deceased, and at one point had to glance down at his notes to ensure he had the right name. As he whipped through the long list of standard platitudes the widow sobbed quietly, the children sat motionless, and the ten or twelve real mourners who had poured through the doors looked bored. Several amused themselves by counting the lights in the ceiling, there were twelve, or counting the floral displays around the casket, there were four. All appeared relieved when the Benediction was given and the coffin wheeled away to the furnace.

The two policemen sat near the back of the small chapel so they could make a quick exit during those few minutes when no one wants to be the first to stand and make their getaway.

Once outside they positioned themselves in a spot providing a clear view of the entire front area of the building and Lou's camera started to click as the ten or twelve mourners poured out. Will kept himself busy scribbling down the names of all the media types he knew in the crowd. If anything was to strike him as strange or was somehow not quite right, he knew there would be plenty of pictures and videos to call upon for backup.

He also noted no authors or any of the Crafty Press suppliers or customers were there. There was no library representative and no one from the local arts council, or any other literary organization. The only ones who cared enough to be present were a few family members, and most looked to be from the wife's side. Will shook his head as he made notes. It all seemed a little unreal.

On the way back to the station he asked Lou if he had ever been to a funeral as weird as the one they had just attended.

"No, I can't say as I have. I almost felt sorry for the guy but then I figure that blonde babe made it sound so good, anyone seeing her report would think this funeral was a smashing success."

His words just made Will feel more depressed.

Chapter Fifteen

Colin Fraser sat at his desk with his two top detectives opposite.

"Okay guys, it's been eight days and now is the time to tell me what you've got and who we'll arrest within the next few days."

Will had gone through this type of routine many times over the years and he was well prepared. Reaching to his feet he extracted a file folder from his briefcase and flipped it open on his lap.

"Well boss, this is the wackiest murder case I've ever worked. Usually we have to first find a motive. That's not necessary in this case because everyone has a motive. We have a multitude that worked with him or for him or did business with him and all hated him with a passion. So far he's described as a drunk, a womanizer, a no good unscrupulous bastard and a cheap cheat. And those are just the nice things they say about him. It's like a competition on who hates him the most and all say they didn't kill him but they certainly have wanted to at some time in the past."

Handing Colin the folder, he continued. "We also have some very unsavory people who lent him money and may have knocked him off as an example. On top of all that we have several husbands around town who are pretty sure he was banging their wives. Now that's a motive if I ever saw one."

"We still have a couple of authors to interview. One's in Cuba with his brother doing research, the other is on vacation. They're both due back soon so we'll get on them this weekend." Will handed his boss a three page summary of their efforts. "These are the details" was all he added.

Collin shuffled enthusiastically through the papers in the folder, flicked it shut and tossed it back to Will. He knew from experience that the wily old Scot not only did a thorough job of reporting, he also knew every trick in the book to cover his ass when it might need covering.

"I hope you guys know there's a little pressure from on high to get this one put to bed, soon. The longer we take, the more bizarre the theories coming out will be. The Mayor told me a reporter from a small Toronto rag called suggesting the hit was by a Mexican drug cartel because Jefferson was about to release an explosive new book describing the cartels operations in Canada."

"I assured him it was a load of crap but these types of stories are going to come fast and furious if this thing keeps poking along at a snail's pace." Collin leaned back to stretch before continuing.

"So now we have a hundred good reasons why lots of people would like to see him dead and at least twenty of them capable of the deed. We also have two moderately good detectives who are going to have to use their heads and some good old fashioned seat of the pants detective work to solve this. To help you along like the great leader I am, I'll pass on one more tidbit of information. Forensics feel there's a better than even chance our killer was left handed."

"Bloody hell" Will roared, "What do you mean 'moderately good' detectives? We're the best you have, the very best" and he turned to Lou. "I've never been so insulted, did ye no hear him? He said 'moderately good'. I think I should be calling the union and filing a grievance."

Lou, laughing, waved Will away. "More like a good old fashioned drawing and quartering if you ask me, maybe with a pot of boiling oil thrown in. Isn't that what you blue faced barbarians did when you got a little pissed off?"

The meeting was now over and Will was on his feet, briefcase in hand. "You two can sit here and make all the bloody jokes you want" he sniffed. "I have some good old fashioned detective work to do finding a left handed killer and I can't stand around chatting with you two dumbbells" and he marched from the room accompanied by Collin and Lou's badly hummed rendition of Scotland the Brave.

Chapter Sixteen

The balance of the day, and most of the next, was spent checking facts and gathering the almost limitless number of details that made up the life of the deceased.

Mrs. Jefferson e-mailed a list of all books published over the past three years and included a list of all those about to be published or somewhere in the process of being prepared for publication. The list included three new authors. He wasn't at all surprised to learn that none of the unpublished tomes had anything to do with drugs coming in from Mexico or any other place. Will made a note to send that information on to Collin.

The bank Crafty Press used was more than happy to co-operate by supplying the company records for the last four years while the wife handed over every monthly credit card statement for five years. She did all the accounting work for both the company and family and was more than willing to supply anything they asked for. He and Lou went through it all with a fine tooth comb but came up empty. It was all it should be, including tax reporting and HST trust funds. Mrs. Jefferson was very efficient.

Lou strolled into Will's office at this point and slipped two sheets of paper onto Will's desk. "Take a look at these" he said.

"What's this all about?" his partner asked.

"This is the report on the victim's personal computer found in his car during the crime scene search. It says there is a large section of memory buried and inaccessible and our computer whiz kids don't have the expertise to unlock it. They suggest we send the laptop to the Provincial Police forensic lab in Orillia for further examination."

Will looked over the report and asked Lou if he thought it important.

"Hell yes. I think our victim was hiding something he was bent on keeping anyone from having a look at. Our guys figure it's some little known form of double encryption to keep snoopy noses out. He says it could take him weeks to work it out so we should send it north. He claims they have some very sophisticated new programs capable of decoding this type of thing quickly and we should have some answers within days." Lou took the report and turned to leave.

"Tell the geeks they did a good job and ask Collin if he can arrange a uniform to get this up to Orillia as quickly as possible. You never know what surprises may be hidden in there. And another thing Lou, we've got two appointments with two authors in Mississauga. One is Pommeroy, Albert Pommeroy, the other, a guy by the name of Winston Rhule, so let's try and get out of here between one-thirty and one-forty-five." Lou waved as he left without turning back or stopping.

Will spent the next hour organizing his notes and files and getting his thoughts on the case in order. He was slowly getting a handle on this one, but he wanted to interview the rest of those on his list before aiming at anyone. In his mind he was positive the robbery was rigged, the work of someone who wanted it to look like a mugging gone bad. In his years on the street and in homicide he had seldom seen a robbery victim cleaned out of everything the way Peter Jefferson had been. It didn't ring true.

Having come to the conclusion it was a planned murder by someone wanting it to look like a smash and grab, he now had to figure out who hated the publisher the most and was capable of doing the dirty deed. He made a note to check the titles of the books Crafty Press put out to see if any were murder mysteries. What the hell, you never know he thought.

Chapter Seventeen

Lou drove toward Mississauga for the first of two interviews while Will thumbed through what little they had on their next author. He was a Jamaican born writer of children's books by the name of Winston Rhule.

Mr. Rhule's family had immigrated to Canada when he was a teenager and according to Will's notes, he had done quite well for himself. He was married and living with his wife and two grown children in a home he owned in Erin Mills, one of Mississauga's better areas. The home was free of any mortgage and according to the Municipal Property Assessment Corporation of Ontario was worth well over half a million dollars.

He had no criminal record and his only brush with the law was a speeding ticket in North Toronto more than a decade ago. Mr. Rhule did not seem to be the type of person who went around sticking pens in people.

Will had leafed through a copy of Winston's latest effort given to them by Mrs. Jefferson entitled *'Vegetables Are Your Friends'.* At about twenty to thirty pages long, Rhule's prose was directed to those between the ages of three and six. The book had lots of large vegetable pictures with smiley faces and names like Tomato Tom and Avocado Allen involved in a story made up of short sentences. Will suggested it might be the kind of book Lou would want to read but his helpful offering just earned him a dirty look.

"This is probably a wild goose chase" Will said as they turned onto Erin Mills Parkway. "This guy is clean. He worked at the Ontario Food Terminal for twenty eight years fork-lifting Florida lettuce and California peppers onto delivery trucks. Then he retired and started writing books for kids. You really have to wonder how someone makes that kind of a transition."

Turning off the Parkway into the residential area Lou commented on the size and outward appearance of the homes they were passing. "I wonder what paid for a home in this place, lifting lettuce or writing books."

"Probably the lettuce" said Will. "From what I can tell not too many of the writers we've seen are living high off the hog. Anyway, we can ask him because that's his place" and pointed to a house looking like its owner loved it.

Winston's home was a standard Greenpark creation similar to hundreds of others in the Erin Mills section of Mississauga. It had four bedrooms up, a large double garage dominating the front and the standard double driveway. Over the years each of these almost identical homes had received enough updates to make the sameness disappear. Now the street was lined with beautiful homes reflecting many different personalities.

The garage door was open and as they approached a booming island accent rolled down the driveway, engulfing them.

"Come on in. I'm having a beer and fixing my lawn mower." The owner of the voice was as black as coal and sported a head of long salt and pepper braids. His gray-tinged full beard was split by the whitest and brightest smile Will had ever seen and he was holding a Red Stripe bottle in one hand. "Want one?" he asked, still ginning.

"Not right now" waved Lou "although I may come back after work and take you up on the offer. I was in Negril once, drank a truckload of it, good beer that."

"Here, sit down" their host said and pulled out a couple of lawn chairs. "I'm sure you have some questions about my publisher and we might as well be comfortable."

"Sure do" Will said, slipping easily into a good mood.

"Then ask away, I'm all ears."

"Okay, where were you when Mr. Jefferson died?"

"Kingston Jamaica mon, getting ready to come back, two days later I was on a plane for home."

"Do you mind telling us what you were doing there?" Lou asked.

"Irie mon, can't you tell I was born there" he laughed. "I go back often. My dad still lives there as well as lots of aunts, uncles and cousins. I fly down a couple times a year to recharge my batteries.

Will changed the subject, "How did you get along with Peter Jefferson?"

"Just fine, he and I were the best of friends. In fact he loved over-proof white rum and I always brought him a bottle of Wray and Nephews when I came back from the island. It's the best there is and at a hundred and fifty proof, unavailable up here."

"You never had any problems with him?" Will asked.

"Hell no mon, he and I were the best of buddies. I know others hated him but not me, I liked him."

"How odd" Lou mused. "I wonder why the difference."

"Money my friend, money, I made him a lot of money. I have the same arrangements as all his other writers, but my books sold. My first book, 'Escape from the Soup Bowl', was a hit. Sold over ten thousand copies, it did, and when I suggested that was it, that I could write no more, that's when he became my best friend. He helped me, prodded me and begged me to write more. I did and the rest is history. My books are now translated into four or five languages, shipped all over the world and have made us both a lot of money, and I mean a lot." Winston sat back in his lawn chair and sucked on his Red Stripe, quite pleased with himself.

"How did you ever come to write a children's book?" Lou asked.

"You mean how did a street kid from the toughest section of Spanish Town come to Canada, spend most of his life slugging produce at the local warehouse, end up writing a kid's book?" he laughed with a deep wonderful rumble and slowly shook his head from side to side. "Grandchildren, they're to blame."

"My wife and daughter left me one day to mind my four year old granddaughter and she drove me nuts trying to get me to tell her a story. I couldn't find anything to read to her and I didn't know any stories, so to shut her up I had to invent one." Winston smiled.

"So I told her about two tomatoes, a boy and a girl, who escaped from the produce terminal after a rotten rutabaga said they were headed for a soup pot in a restaurant. He said they were to be cooked to a squishy mess and finally garnished with Bill Basil. The story was a big hit with her and the next day she clamored for more stories about 'begibles' as she called them." At this point he reached into a cooler for another beer.

"My wife originally copied the tales into a note book so our daughter could read them to the child at home. She later convinced me to send them to a publisher. I did and as the saying goes 'the rest is history'."

Lou shook his head and looked over at Will who sat viewing Winston with a look of respect.

"You say you made a lot from these books?" Will asked. "I'm curious and it has nothing to do with our investigation, would you mind giving me an idea of just what a lot is?"

"Not at all, Pete had asked me to keep it quiet but now that he's gone, what difference can it make. My total book sales last year were about thirty-five thousand units and I made over a dollar fifty a unit in royalties. It's all in the tax returns I file, so there was no fiddling."

"That's well over fifty thousand just last year" Will said to a broadly smiling Winston Rhule. "What will you do now that he's gone?"

Again the writer laughed "Hell, I've been fighting off agents wanting to represent me since I returned from Jamaica. Don't you worry none, I'll have no problems publishing my stories."

"Good for you" said Will as he stood, "I wish you great success."

They all shook hands and Winston walked with them down the driveway to their car. Will liked the man. He was one of those stories that made all their efforts worthwhile, sort of like sweet icing on what was usually a dung cake. It was nice to meet Peter Jefferson's only truly successful author and probably one of the few people outside his family who didn't hate his guts.

Chapter Eighteen

The other author on their Mississauga list lived in a condo on Eglinton Avenue. It was one of the many ten or twelve story monstrosities built around Toronto in the 1980's and 90's, most with less architectural appeal than a sewage treatment plant, but generally not as much smell.

Albert Pommeroy opened the door when they knocked, coughed twice and casually waved them in.

"Come in gentlemen" Mr. Pommeroy said as he held the door for them. "I just got back and found out what has transpired. It's a great shock. Come in, let's talk" and he ushered them into his living room.

The man looked like a writer if writers had a special look. He was slender, not quite six feet tall and wore a two day growth of beard. The cigarette hanging from the corner of his mouth sported an inch of drooping ash looking for a clear spot on the carpet to target. Although half way through the afternoon, Albert Pommeroy was in slippers, pajamas and open full-length dressing robe with its sash dragging along behind. Will wondered if Raymond Chandler dressed like this in the afternoon.

"Can I get you guys anything?" he asked as they sat down.

"We're fine" Will said and took out his notebook.

"Okay, let's get on with it then. What do you want to know?"

"We understand you're under contract to Crafty Press" Lou started.

"Three years now" Pommeroy coughed.

Lou continued "how has the relationship been?"

"No real problem. He was great at first, then tried to flex his muscles and push me around. I told him he was stepping out of line and he got abusive. I then told him he might regret treating me badly. Well, he then got mouthy and more abusive so I sued him." He sat back in his chair, coughed a couple more times and lit another cigarette with an old Zippo flip top lighter.

"What were the grounds for the lawsuit?" Will asked.

"It's a 'Breach of Contract' suit. He produced a substandard product that I paid for, and I sued him for producing a defect."

"How is the suit going?" Will again.

"He was stalling and dodging and doing a double shuffle legally, but no matter how long it takes or how much time gets wasted, when all is said and done, he'll be the loser, his crappy company will be a loser and I'll be the winner." He confidently swung his head away from his self-produced cloud of smoke and some ashes fell onto his pajamas.

Lou asked the next question. "Is your contract similar to all the others, you're in for life and unless you win this lawsuit you either publish through Crafty Press or not at all?"

"You got it right on one point. It is a lifetime contract and if I win, I'm free. Now if I lose, I just publish using another name and another publisher, that's all. It may bother some you know, writers sitting on huge egos, but not me. I write for the money and as long as my books get published and they send me the checks, I don't give a damn what name is on the cover."

"I would assume you have no new books coming out during this fight, how do you survive during this long legal battle?" Lou asked.

"I'm a writer. I write. I can sell as many as five articles or feature stories a month and they range from three hundred to fifteen hundred bucks each. There are thousands of monthly, weekly and even daily publications out there that need quality writers who can meet a deadline. Don't worry about me, I get by."

"How does this tragedy affect your lawsuit?" Will asked.

"First off, it's no tragedy. I would think there are loads of people who have been dancing in the street since they heard the good news. For my part, I don't think it affects me at all. He and his company are co-defendants in my lawsuit. Now that he's gone, it still stands against the company. If whoever is running Crafty Press wants me to go away, they can give me an iron clad release from that shitty contract and I'll withdraw the suit and disappear into the sunset. Otherwise, it's off to court we go."

The three men sat quietly as Lou jotted down these details in his notebook with Will just sitting and looking at the man across from him light another cigarette. Finally Will broke the silence in the room with a series of short questions.

"You were away on holidays these past few days were you not?"

"Yes, well actually, a working holiday. I was doing some research for a travel article I'm working on but I have to admit my brother was with me and there was a lot of holidaying involved" Albert replied with a chuckle.

"Where did you leave from, where did you go and exactly when did you leave?"

"We flew from Toronto to Havana on Air Canada and if what I read in the papers is right, the much hated Mr. Jefferson bit the dust about one a.m. My brother and I left about six hours later 'cause our flight went out at seven o'clock. I guess I missed all the excitement and joy but I've sure followed all the news of that evening's events since I got back. If you like I can produce all the bills and receipts. It was a working vacation and the tax department just loves those little details."

"One last question" Will asked quietly. "Where were you and what were you doing during the evening before you left for Cuba?"

"Here, packing, having a few drinks and getting everything ready. With the bloody security at the airports these days you have to be there at least two hours before flight time. So I figured leaving here about four, delivering my car to my usual off airport parking lot and being in the terminal with lots of time to spare. It worked out pretty well and it was a nice flight. Actually the whole trip was pretty nice and the icing on the cake was the good news about Jefferson when I got back. All in all it has been a good couple of weeks." Again Pommeroy lit another cigarette.

Both Will and Lou asked a few more minor questions before closing their notebooks and standing. Albert rose through the smoke, emerging into the semi-clean air to join them in the slow walk to the condo's door.

"If there's anything else I can do for you guys just let me know. Peter was a shit, there's no doubt of that but one hates to see anyone cut down in a back alley behind some crummy bar, especially with his own pen. Call me if you need me" he said as he opened the door for them.

"We will Mr. Pommeroy. Please let us know if you go off on another of your working vacations." Lou said as he handed the writer one of his cards.

"Nothing planned" Albert grinned and waved to them as they made their way down the hallway. Neither man looked back or said anything until the elevator's doors slid shut.

"What do you think?" Lou asked.

"I wonder how he knew Jefferson was killed by his own pen. I don't think it was ever said it was the victim's pen. It's my feeling this bears some further study, as they say at Scotland Yard" Will smiled grimly at his young partner. "You do know what Scotland Yard is, I hope."

"Of course I do ya haggis eater" Lou scoffed. "It's the same as a German Yard, thirty-six inches long."

Chapter Nineteen

Before Lou slipped the car into gear he reset the trip calculator button sticking from the speedometer.

"Maybe we should check the time and distance between here and the bar in Dundas" he said.

"Good thinking" Will grunted, not looking up from his interview notes. He said little while Lou worked his way down the 403 and onto the QE highway but as they neared the exit to Hamilton he asked "Did you get any twitches with that guy?"

"I sure as hell did. That's why I thought we'd check how much time it takes to drive from the condo to the bar. There's probably a record of his arrival at the parking lot as well. I've the feeling he may have had enough time to play bad guy that night."

"Could be" Will mused. "He was a little too laid back, too under control to be real. I got the feeling he thought he was playing a role in an old Humphrey Bogart movie. My sixth sense says he wasn't telling us the whole truth most of the time."

"I had the same feeling. When we get back to the station I'll run a deep check on him and see what we come up with. I'll also get his phone records. The preliminary report says he's clean but a little more effort could bring something up."

Lou pulled onto Main Street West and drove past the huge medical centre toward Dundas. They would soon know if Mr. Albert Pommeroy had time to drive from Mississauga to the bar in Dundas and back to the airport to catch his plane for Cuba.

They finished their drive in silence, each going over the facts now falling into place. Lou pulled into the alley that led onto the back parking area behind the bar and looked at the clock on the dash, calculating the time.

"Fifty-five minutes in medium traffic so let's call it an hour. If he kept within the speed limit so as not to attract attention, it's an easy hour to the bar and an easy hour back home. He lives about fifteen minutes from the airport so let's call his driving time two and a half hours at the most. Add to this about an hour for his setup time. Doing things like parking his car, getting his two by four from the trunk, finding an appropriate spot to wait for Jefferson. Then we add on the actual attack time and pocket emptying time. I'd say you have no more than four hours, tops, maybe quite a bit less." Lou tapped the numbers in his notebook to conclude.

Will climbed from the car as Lou got out and stood looking around. "So let's figure this out" he said. "Pommeroy knows Jefferson is a champion drinker and never left a bar before closing time unless to jump some girl he picked up. He also knows this is Jefferson's favorite watering hole because of the two or three beauties who work here. He would arrive around twelve thirty and start to set up. This would mean he left the condo between eleven and eleven thirty." Will was now walking around the lot behind the bar as he spoke,

"Pommeroy recognizes Jefferson's car, knows he's in the bar and gets ready to meet him. Our man staggers out shortly after one, Pommeroy whacks him and our publisher falls to the ground. I'd think Pommeroy brought a bag with him so he starts emptying pockets to make it look like a robbery. During these minutes Jefferson may have started to come around while his assailant was down on one knee examining the pen. In a moment of panic or rage or both, Pommeroy slams his fist down, jamming the nib of the pen into Jefferson's neck. Total time he would need to do all this, no less than three but no more than five minutes. Hell, our Mr. Pommeroy could have done the dirty on Jefferson and been back in his condo by two thirty."

Lou nodded "it certainly fits together, doesn't it. I think he has the makings of a real live suspect."

"Young man, you're right. T'would seem as though some of my hard work and brilliant teaching in things investigative have become embedded in your wee brain" Will said with a grin. Lou ignored him.

"You have his brother's name and number along with the name of his parking lot so let's check that out. He drives a black Mercedes so let's have another look at the bar security tapes. I know they show nothing of the attack but they might show a dark car cruising by. Look into that. When we get back to the office I'll start going over his phone calls, you call the airport to get their security tapes and we'll check when he and his brother walked into departures."

Heading back to the car Will rubbed his hands together, giving Lou a wicked grin. "Let's get a move on Watson. The games afoot" he declared in excitement.

Chapter Twenty

Piecing together every minute in the time line of a suspect's life takes endless hours and a great deal of patience. Constant review and tedious back checking of events, stories and facts is required.

The airline confirmed Albert Pommeroy was indeed on their plane, as was his brother, and in fact both had checked in at the counter in Pearson's Terminal One at precisely 5:11. Boarding started at 6:40, so that portion of time was locked in.

Will informed Collin Fraser he thought they were on to something and asked for a junior for his team to help with the paper work. Within an hour a perky new member of the force stood at his desk in her crisp new uniform, asking eagerly for her first duties. Will obliged and sent her off, blonde ponytail a-bobbing, on her first job. He had asked her to take a car and carefully redo the trip from Pommeroy's home to the bar and back, once at mid-day and again that evening at eleven.

The next morning at exactly nine A.M. the pretty five foot four bundle of energy stood again at his desk, presenting her perfectly listed routing between Pommeroy's condo and the Dundas bar, all done in minutes and seconds. The report also included the routes and times between the suspect's home and the parking lot he used just off the airport grounds and contained the average time the parking lot operator took to get their customers to and from the airport.

Will looked up at her from his desk and tapped the spreadsheets with his finger "What did you do lassie, use a stop watch?"

"Yes" she smiled and pulled one from her pocket. "My father gave it to me when I joined the force. He said if I was accurate, I'd impress people."

"Your father is a very wise man. Tell me, is he a Scot?"

"Ukrainian-Italian sir, but he always says your countrymen make great booze, better than vodka."

"See, I knew he was a wise man. Are you sure he hasn't few drams of Scottish blood in his veins? Tell me, is he still around?"

"Oh yes sir. He lives here in town, I often see him."

Will sat back and looked at her. "The next time you talk to that wise old man of yours tell him thank you from me for sending us such a good new police officer."

Beaming, the young policewoman blushed, did a smart about face and proudly left her superior.

Lou came through the door shortly after and asked "What's with 'Tash? She looks like she was walking on air."

"Natasha is her name and she handed me a report that makes yours look like the scribbling of the village idiot. She's good and you may end up heading a team with her as your partner or even superior." Will smiled.

"What an improvement that would be. For one thing she smells one hell of a lot better than you. For another she looks better too, but hell, everybody looks better than you. I'd like that partnership arranged for next week if possible, eh!" Lou shot back as he handed over a report on the laptop found in the victim's car.

"Here, take a look at this" he said.

Will sat and read the report and whistled. It explained how some very sophisticated code was used to hide information from nosy people and a bit about how Orillia had deciphered it. It seems Peter Jefferson had a 'lock and hide' piece of freeware on his computer. It not only allows you to lock folders and drive partitions, but also allows you to do this even when the folders option is set to 'show hidden files and folders'. Without all the brains at the OPP forensic labs in Orillia, the hidden folders would have remained invisible.

The second page listed in point form what was on the drive and set out the procedure for looking at it. Will knew from the list of contents they had a gold mine of activities, possibly nefarious ones, that would complicate their investigation.

"It lists credit card accounts, e-mail addresses, phone numbers, bank accounts and lots of other things. Hell, he even has a mail box at a UPS store in the West End. Have you checked any of this?"

"Just a little" Lou said. "None of the credit card numbers jive with what his wife supplied. Nor the bank accounts. I think we should send 'Tash, sorry, Natasha to the UPS store to see if they'll let us empty the box without a warrant. They might if it isn't some tight-ass running the place. It could prove to be interesting."

"Make it so" Will ordered in his best Jean Luc Picard accent.

"The other thing is his phone book. Almost every name is female. Our boy seemed to have moved on a fast track when it came to women."

Will thought for a moment, deciding on a course of action. "When Natasha gets back have her go through the phone book and check out each name. It will be interesting to know how many are married and maybe ask them how they got on a publishers list."

"You work on the financial end, the credit cards, bank accounts and the stuff Natasha might get from the mail box. If you need help, ask her to jump in. I doubt you'll find that a bad thing." Will was looking at him with a raised eyebrow.

"What an assignment" Lou groaned. "I always said you Scots were tough." and smiling, he left the office humming a tune.

Will sat a long time quietly reading and re-reading the report on the secret files buried in the computer, considering how this may change everything. He already had a good suspect, or someone who could easily have done Jefferson in, and had enough reason to do it, and now this. The secret life of a much hated publisher with what could be many signposts pointing to other people.

Picking up the phone he made a call.

"Lou, how fast can we get a copy of everything in that hidden section of the hard drive?"

"It's already done. See, I'm just as efficient as our new young helper. I'll print it out and have it in your hand in five minutes. Fast enough?"

"Three would be better but I guess it'll have to do. I'm going home to sit by the pool with a cool one and go over this. We may be on to something a lot more different than we first thought. You guys keep working, and another thing, keep this stuff about his other life quiet. There's no reason to tell his wife about this side of him if it means nothing in the end."

"Okay boss" was Lou's answer.

Chapter Twenty-One

The computer files were a revelation.

The secret life that Peter Jefferson had locked away in a corner of his hard drive was a whole lot different than the life the public saw, and it was organized in great detail, making it easy to work through.

He did his banking in three different places in Hamilton. There was a Credit Union account and two bank accounts, one in US dollars. The Canadian dollar accounts each had a few hundred in them, but there were several thousand in the US account.

He had two secret credit cards, a MasterCard from some obscure banking system on the internet, and a Visa card from the Credit Union. Both had lots of room and both showed the mailing address to be the postal box Lou had mentioned.

He had an extensive address book with names, phone numbers and e-mail addresses, most of which Will had not heard of during the early part of the investigation.

The entries included a 'comments' file, with observations about everyone he came into contact. Some caustic comments were short, while others were quite long and detailed. Going over them helped Will better understand why Mister Jefferson was so hated. His only nice comments centered on the breast size of every woman he met. He liked well-endowed girls, but could muster up a few nice things to say about those less developed if they pleased him in other ways or performed special services. The guy was a real piece of work.

After long years as a policeman, both on the street or where he was now, Will knew if you had any brains at all, you quickly picked up on the small signals and signs that guided you in cases.

Some made you shudder and left you wondering about the madness in the world.

Other cases made you angry, infuriating you to the point where logical calm investigation techniques became difficult. These cases often involved children, or the elderly, and were the most gut wrenching, often forcing you to step back and wonder whether you could handle them properly.

Still other cases involved perpetrators you knew were evil bastards, bad guys who become a prize to hunt down and catch, then help convict. You took great pleasure in tracking them, collecting the evidence that would put them away, and finally snapping the cuffs on them, knowing you were cleaning some rubbish off the streets.

This one was totally different. This was the type of case where you had a great deal more sympathy for the perpetrator than you did for the victim. The trouble was you still had to catch the killer, gather as much evidence as possible for the prosecution and constantly work toward a conviction. It had to be done but there would be little satisfaction in its successful completion.

Sitting next to his pool with a stiff drink close at hand, Will sifted through the 'comments'. In them he found one notation simply saying 'the stupid bitch Drew sent another letter. I wonder sometimes if that old hag will ever die'. Nice, thought Will.

Another, written in caps said 'Cindy called. What a pair of knockers she has. She's one of the few who look better naked than clothed. Wants a get together, can't wait.' Will made a note of the date of that one for cross checking with the list of women Natasha was going through. He'd ask her to check the credit card bills and see if there was a charge for a hotel around then. Maybe something might come up.

There was one notation about what Peter called 'the crazy old fool of a Russian bastard in Montreal', at least three about 'that son of a bitch Pommeroy and his lawsuit' and another two about MacDonald, the writer who had been in hospital for the past five weeks. Even these were as nasty as the others. It seemed to Will that Mr. Jefferson had little good to say about anyone he couldn't con into a bed for a jump.

The phone next to him rang and he answered "Deas here."

"It's Lou. I have some more on those computer files and a secondary report from forensics. Whatever was used to hit him was definitely flat, like a board, you know, a two by four or even a two by six, something like that. It was not a pipe or a hammer or a tire iron, or something round or with sharp edges. How's that for an interesting fact?"

"Were there any wood fibers in his hair?"

"Nope, there was nothing. Whatever was used to bash him was flat, clean and left no residue."

"I did a case many years ago where a guy's head was bashed in with a shovel. Maybe we should be looking for an author who writes gardening books."

"Very droll" was all Lou could muster.

"What about the computer files?" Will asked.

"They go back a long way, right to the time he bought the thing. It seems to be a diary or journal of some sort. Henry Lee in Tech claims the computer ran with two systems at the same time. He said the operator could be sitting working in Excel or Word and anyone looking over his shoulder would see that. Then with a click he could be into his secondary section, the one with the firewalls stopping snoopers from entering. Lee said it was a method used only by people with something to hide. He also said it was pretty slick and could only be installed by someone who knew computers well."

"Have you heard anything from Natasha?"

There was a short pause before Lou answered. "Actually she was just in here to give me an update on her research. She's very good and had a superb report even though it was an interim one."

"And she has great legs too, eh?" Will offered.

"Give me a break, will you! I hadn't even noticed but with you mentioning it, I know I'm sure to look the next time she's in. Damn, next you'll be telling me she has a pretty face and I'll have to check that out as well."

"I know poor boy, but hey, you knew this was a tough job when you joined, so just suck it up and get on with it. No one ever promised you a rose garden" and Will held the phone for a few seconds before hanging up so Lou could hear his laughing.

Chapter Twenty-Two

Lou hung up with a broad grin and sat reflecting on his partner. He knew the wily old Scot recognized and appreciated a beautiful woman when he saw one and he also knew he was a tease, a provocateur and a good judge of character. Lou guessed his partner had seen his eyes following Natasha as she moved about the station, and why not, she was nice to look at. He chuckled as he rose from his desk to visit Henry Lee in Tech. Henry had left a message to call back but the young detective figured he'd walk up and visit personally, thinking he would have to pass Natasha's work area to get there. That thought put a little extra spring in his step.

His partner was an old fox and Lou knew it. Will called himself a grass widow, a man who had been married but now wasn't. The truth was Will's wife had left him. Margaret Deas, or Maggie to all who knew her, was a person you might call of good peasant stock whose ancestors had been crofters in the Highlands of Scotland. During the clearances they were driven from the land and over the next couple of centuries drifted in search of food and work until they settled in Glasgow. She was short, a little overweight though not obese, and her family was her life.

Charming and pleasant, Maggie Deas was capable of entertaining the best the town had to offer but she was in the end a homebody.

Will's wife considered special occasions like birthdays, anniversaries and all the various religious holidays the reason for existing, and his police work interfered with this view of the world and caused great hardship in their relationship. Maggie never accepted the idea that a cop was on call twenty-four hours a day, seven days a week.

He was a policeman first, always and forever and his wife never could understand that. For twenty years she argued and pleaded with him to ignore the call, demanding he have someone else respond. She never understood that her husband didn't like leaving in the middle of a dinner party to look at a dead body, but felt obligated to do so. She finally decided she couldn't go on so she bundled up the kids and left him. After all those years she sat and poured her heart out in a long letter, sealed it, and stuck it on the refrigerator with a magnet.

There was a reticence amongst Will's co-workers to discuss their comrade's private life, and it had taken Lou a long time to find out the details of Will's failed marriage. The Scot never spoke of it and Lou left it alone, but he knew Mrs. Deas was still Mrs. Deas and she communicated with Will through phone or email, usually about their grown children or three grandchildren.

The stroll through the halls and up the stairs to Henry Lee's workshop took several minutes and took several extra when Lou accidentally bumped into

Officer Natasha Iannini as she hurried along a corridor with a sheaf of papers in her hand.

"Hi" he called to her as she rounded a corner.

Stopping, she turned around and instantly her pretty but serious face broke into a big happy smile. "Hi yourself detective, how are you doing?"

"I'm doing very well indeed and please, call me Lou."

Laughing she said "Okay Lou but only if you call me Natasha. Deal?" and she stuck out her free hand.

"Deal" he said taking her hand, maybe holding it a little bit longer than normal. Both moved quietly in the direction she had been going, giving each a chance to adjust to the delightful tension in the air, not wanting to say anything to endanger this new thing.

"How's our murder investigation going?" she finally asked.

"Pretty good. Will is at home with a tall cool drink going over a transcript of the victim's computer notes."

"Does he do that often?" she asked.

"What, go home to read, yea, whenever he wants peace and quiet and he's thinking about a case and trying to sort things out in his head. In the summer he'll sit by his pool and sip scotch with his cat curled up on his lap. During the winter he holes up in his den, or library you might call it, starts a real fire and sits by it, again sipping and puffing on that stinky old pipe of his."

"Ugh, the idea of a pipe just turns me off" Natasha shuddered.

"Oh it's not all that bad. We just make fun of him and his pipe. I'm getting so I kind of like the smell. Whenever I visit him at home it's like stepping back in time. My dad and grandfather both smoked a pipe." Lou defended his partner. "It's a lot like cooking. When you enter a home where the lady of the house is making soup or baking cookies the smell sweeps you back to a nicer time. It's the same with Will's pipe."

"My mom still cooks wearing an apron covered with flour in a large kitchen where everyone gathers." Natasha said. "When you open the door you're hit with a wave of wonderful aromas. You sure as heck know a member of an older generation is busy making something. Maybe you're right about the lingering smell, maybe sometime you'll have to take me to Detective Deas' home and I'll stand quietly with my eyes closed and just sniff the air. I might like it."

Their last few steps before parting were in comfortable silence and when she turned right to go her way they simply smiled at each other and said 'see ya' and both knew it would be so.

Chapter Twenty-Three

There were only a few more authors who Will and Lou hadn't interviewed, and they were well on their way to getting them done.

Jan Henning was next on their list. She had been away in Egypt acting as escort to a gang of old folk intent on spending as much of their children's inheritance as quickly as they could. She worked full time in a travel organization specializing in tours for seniors, or in the modern vernacular, those in their golden years. At least that's what the agency's brochure said, and Will was not one to argue with brochures, although he figured 'in your golden years' meant you were the one with the gold that everyone else wanted.

Jan got all the gory details of Peter Jefferson's death from her work mates the morning after her return from the Nile. They also told her the police wanted to talk to her on her return so she called to let them know she was back in town and available. She knew they'd get around to her eventually.

Ms. Henning, a vivacious party girl in her early years was now a vivacious party girl in her mid-fifty's. She started her work career as a young slip of a thing with a small regional carrier running a regular scheduled service out of Hamilton airport to exciting places like Ottawa, Windsor and Pittsburgh. She wowed the mostly bored male passengers as they moved through the airport, becoming well known to regulars who traveled. Eventually the airline was sold and despite her good looks and nice legs, she ended up looking for another job. She finally got her present one in a travel agency where she became their chief guide and escort. Since she loved to travel, it was a perfect match.

Jan had a knack for telling funny stories about her charges and at the suggestion of some friends expanded into writing travel articles for local dailies and a chain of weekly papers. It wasn't long before she was writing for several glossy magazines across the country.

Her style was funny, her stories slightly bizarre, and the locales interesting and exotic. These elements made her first full book about travel a sure hit even when published by a halfwit, which she soon learned her publisher was.

Lou drove down Bay Street to York Boulevard and swung onto the parking lot of a small office building containing restaurants, small shops, and Jan's travel agency. Will remembered it as the former home of a radio station where he visited to give an interview about the very first murder case he had ever been assigned. A young reporter just out of a community college journalism course did the interview and asked some of the dumbest questions Will had ever heard, before or since. In exasperation he explained to the novice what a murder was, and told him to go back to school, stay awake and listen to the teacher. The reporter turned out to be the station owner's son. It resulted in the only letter regarding rudeness ever filed against him and taught him not to lose his temper in the face of blatant stupidity.

All five foot two of Jan was waiting for them so the formalities of introduction took only a minute. She was not a lady to waste time on social niceties or small talk so after a firm handshake Ms. Henning was ready for of immediate action. She walked back around her desk, slipped into her chair and stared at the two detectives with the largest and darkest eyes Will had ever seen.

"What would you like to know?" she demanded.

"Well Ms. Henning," Will started, "we would like to hear all you know about Peter Jefferson."

"Hell, if you want to hear everything I know about him you'd better have one hell of a lot of time. What I know about that son-of-a-bitch can't be told or absorbed in minutes. In fact it may take the rest of the day and part of the night."

Will looked at Lou and knew what he was thinking. They both got out their notebooks and unleashed their pens.

"First off how long did you know him?" Will started.

"Five years. I was one of the early fish he reeled into his scam."

"Have you a lifetime contract with Crafty Press like his other authors?" Lou asked.

"Yes" she stated.

"Did you have to purchase a specific number of books with each publication?"

"You bet. It started out at three hundred and fifty copies but he tried to raise it to five hundred. I fought that and kept it at the lower amount."

"Was that your only problem with him?" Lou asked.

Jan looked at the two policemen and shrugged. "Since he's dead, I guess it doesn't matter what I tell you. He can't hurt me now."

Will had the feeling this girl's relationship with her publisher was different from the other authors and she had been afraid of him. "As long as it's the truth you can tell us and no, he can't hurt you." He was going to add 'anymore' but thought better of it.

"Fine" she said. "First off he was a filthy bastard who couldn't keep his hands off any woman within arms-length. He got slapped a few times but that never stopped him. I raised hell with him once when he ran his hand right up under my skirt. It happened in his office when I delivered a manuscript. Hell, his wife was in the kitchen when it happened."

"I didn't make a fuss but told him quietly if he tried that sort of thing again I'd tell his wife. I heard nothing from him about the book for over a year although our contract said maximum six months for a decision. He would do that to teach you he was boss and had all the power."

"He also was a bad one for doing nothing. I would give him a cheque with my new manuscript, he would have the book printed mistakes and all, then call me to pick up my copies when it was shipped in from the printers. From that point on the little jerk would do nothing, absolutely nothing! He never arranged a single book signing! He never set up a reading! He never once got me an interview on radio or with a newspaper! The little crook just applied for his government grants, shipped a copy to one or two of the large book chains and e-mailed notices to a few websites and catalogs!" Jan was getting wound up, her voice raising and her hands moving in agitation.

"That time, the son-of-a-bitch held my money and my manuscript for over a year, that was the end. I called him almost thirteen months after he got both and he yelled at me to stop bothering him and hung up on me. Can you imagine him saying that? Stop bothering him when I hadn't spoken to the little piece of crap in over a year." Ms. Hennings was angry.

"I called my lawyer and he sent a demand for a refund of my money and my manuscript as per the contract and threatened to sue him if he didn't hear from him in seven days." She was standing now, pacing about her office with fire in her eyes.

"Two days later he called me and was all sweet and conciliatory. I listened politely to his spiel and when he was finished, convinced he had me back in line, I calmly told him to talk to my lawyer and hung up."

"Well he did call my lawyer, not realizing he was talking to a pit bull who would rather sue than have sex. My man beat the jerk to the ground and had him groveling within minutes. He got me a bigger advance and the number of books I had to purchase dropped to one hundred and fifty. The lawyer also made him refund the difference I had paid him."

Lou and Will never opened their mouths. They were content to sit and listen to Jan Henning tear the dead publisher to pieces. Will thought it would be good therapy for her.

"And you want to know something?" Jan continued "That little bastard didn't even have the balls to face me. He sent his poor long suffering wife to my home in Mount Hope with the refund cheque and the one covering the increase in the advance. Imagine, he sent his wife! What a cowardly little fart he was and I'm glad he's dead. In fact I think I'll take the rest of the day off and get drunk in celebration 'cause this world is now a lot better place with him gone."

She sat down, glad to get it all off her chest. Will shook his head and closed his notebook. He knew she wasn't remotely a suspect, having twenty-five gray haired tourists to verify her presence in Egypt with them. Her long testimony only confirmed everything he already knew about the man. He knew they were through with the interview.

"Thank you for your time and the information on your dealings with the victim. It does sound as though he was not a very nice man but even someone as bad as Mr. Jefferson doesn't deserve to be killed in a back alley late at night, as he was" Will said.

Jan stood again, her tailored business suit showing the still lovely curves of her figure and stuck out her hand, shaking her head sadly. "No, I guess you're right. He didn't deserve to be killed in the dark of a back alley behind a second rate bar. The little prick should have been killed in broad daylight, possibly at twelve noon on the front steps of City Hall on Main Street with everyone he ever screwed watching and cheering, That would have been far more fitting!" and she shook Will's hand firmly.

There was no doubt in either policeman's mind as they left that she meant every word she said.

On the way back to the station Lou chuckled and shook his head. "I think that lady has a little of your tough Scots' blood coursing through her veins."

"Ye may be right lad" Will said with his broad 'use only when he felt like it' brogue. "She was a feisty wee lassie, was she not? If she hadn't been wandering around Egypt with so many witnesses I'd put her down as a right good suspect. I can see her whacking him over the head with a fry pan, but I think she may have shoved that pen someplace other than his neck" and they both laughed.

Chapter Twenty-Four

Because of the amount of information on the dead man's laptop, Will assigned Lou and Natasha to try to make some sort of order to the files, sorting them into understandable categories. The younger detective loved working on computers and from the looks he and Natasha were exchanging whenever they were together, he figured they may be able to come up with something useful.

Their chief suspect at this point was Albert Pommeroy, the tough talking Mississauga crime writer. He had the ability and the opportunity but the motive factor was a little thin. Will knew any decent defense lawyer could punch holes in the case they had so far. To make a charge stick on Pommeroy, they would need a lot more solid evidence. Will decided he would work on that while his two underlings sorted through the plethora of possible suspects to see if someone else emerged ahead of Pommeroy.

So far they had uncovered the names and some details of over a dozen females living in or around the city of Hamilton. There were store clerks, hair dressers, waitresses, office workers and stay at home moms. The extensive photo gallery in Jefferson's computer showed they all had several common characteristics. They were all blonde, all wore tight clothes when they were wearing anything, and all seemed happy to pose provocatively. They also had ample bosoms and few inhibitions in showing them. The smiles and come hither looks of their 'selfies' was enough to convince the two detectives that all of the pictures were on the hard drive willingly.

Natasha tracked down the pictures hidden away in a file with the innocuous name of Montmartre Festival, and she was a little shocked at what popped up.

When she showed the pictures to Lou they both looked in silence as the slide show flashed across Natasha's computer monitor. Lou shuffled uncomfortably standing behind Natasha, while she blushed and gasped once or twice. Not much was said other than the photos would have to be cataloged and matched up with the file of names and addresses and then sent to Will for review.

Another file they were making their way through detailed a long list of Government grant and assistance programs, both federal and provincial. The list had dates, amounts, application numbers, and included attached files of application documents. A quick study indicated Jefferson may had lied and cheated on several of them.

There were notes about making sure one author or another knew nothing of the grants from Heritage Canada or the Ontario Arts Council. In several cases cryptic notes were inserted about keeping a particular author away from the others because he was a 'trouble maker'. Most of the data had all the earmarks of a scratch pad or desk blotter onto which someone had jotted down notes and numbers. Will did the same, only it was a desk that was littered with scraps of paper with scribbling on them, not a computer.

As work continued on the investigation, the life of the murdered man emerged as a montage of sordid extramarital activities. There were also some very questionable and immoral dealings with business associates, and outright illegal practices involving Government funds. Will marveled at how long it had taken for someone to kill him. In any other country he would have either been elected President or executed by firing squad.

While his two juniors slogged through their part of the job, Will scrutinized every aspect of Albert Pommeroy's life, looking for something solid. He found nothing. By the end of the day he had the feeling that his prime suspect was not so prime after all. There was nothing about him that fit the profile of a killer. Finally he reached for the phone to ask Lou to bring Natasha to his office for coffee and a chat about the case. It was time for a serious meeting of minds. Within minutes they sat opposite him, Lou happily sipping on his free coffee and Natasha happy to be sitting next to him.

"I've gone over this Pommeroy fellow's file and the more I read the less I think he's our man so I think we have to take a different tact." Will told them.

"I keep wondering why the killer would take his keys and not his car?" he asked them.

"Maybe the killer didn't have time, or maybe he didn't know which car was Jefferson's. There were three or four cars parked out there that night." Lou offered.

"Or maybe he had come to the bar in his own car and couldn't drive two away at once." Natasha suggested.

"That's a real possibility. That would certainly apply to our Mr. Pommeroy, or the old guy in Montreal, or a few others for that matter" Lou added.

"That would open up a whole can of suspects. If we believe the killer drove to the back of the bar, he knew what he was doing; who he was going after, and had an intimate knowledge of the victim's habits. It all comes back to my belief this was a planned killing, not simply a random robbery gone wrong" Will said and sat back to watch his two partners.

Natasha jumped in again "surely it could have been just a robbery."

"No" Will answered "I'm convinced it was not a robbery. It was planned by someone who knew him, knew his movements and took him out exactly the way he wanted. And Natasha, in the words of Canada's greatest detective, Lieutenant Frank Drebin, don't call me Shirley." This broke them all up and caused a few passing heads to turn toward the burst of laughter.

When they had settled down, Will checked his notebook and listed his requirements in the investigation.

"I want you two to put together a suspect list. I want you to include every possible person who might want him dead. I know, I know, it'll be one hell of a long list but I think you guys are up to it." Both the young officers were scribbling in their books.

"When the list is done we're going to start our elimination process and go over every suspect to determine if they had motive, opportunity and ability to be a killer. Some will be easy but don't assume anything, put them on the list. All the authors, all the girlfriends, the loan sharks, the irate husbands, everyone goes on the list. Have it done by this time tomorrow and we'll meet here to start the hard work."

The two slowly stood up looking a bit bewildered. Lou spoke first "Will, this could take all night."

"So, what's your point, get on with it, we've a killer to catch" and he stood, hustling the two out of his office. The young detective and his co-worker headed to the former's office, not looking back at their superior therefore not letting him see the grin each was wearing. Of course their not looking back prevented them from seeing the wide smile on Will's face as he stood in his office doorway, arms folded across his chest.

Chapter Twenty Five

At precisely two the following afternoon a well-dressed Lou and a smartly uniformed Natasha stood at Will's desk holding a multi paged report in a blue three ringed binder. Each had satisfied grins on their face. Lou handed the binder to Will and explained what had been done.

"Here's what you asked for sir, every possible person. The list includes all pertinent details about residence, phones, e-mails and anything else we thought important. We've also included several comments on their alibis if they've been interviewed as well as a ranking system of one to five stars relative to their status as a suspect. One is the lowest level of involvement, such as Ms. Henning who was on her trip to Egypt, and five stars for someone who looks like a real possibility, like our Mr. Pommeroy."

Both stood quietly waiting for a comment with only a slight glance by Natasha up at her fellow officer with something more than a professional glint in her eye.

Will took the binder and slowly opened it, glancing at the columns of facts and figures on the first half dozen pages before he looked up at them and spoke.

"Impressive, very impressive indeed, and I must say you both look very professional and rested after working so hard all night on this. You deserve a great deal of credit for doing such a good job." He stood up and walked around the desk head down, still leafing through the folder. He stopped when in front of them and snapped the binder shut.

"Lou, Natasha, this is very good but it's going to take me several hours to go through it. I'll have to make notes, jot down any questions I may have, and then we'll have to go over it together. I think better at home so I'm going there now and spend the rest of the afternoon doing just that. Notwithstanding your fine appearances, you both must be a little weary and I think you deserve a wee break as well."

Will glanced at his watch and said "Lou, it's now about three, why don't you and Officer Ianinni take the rest of the day off, relax and be back here fresh and bright eyed at eight tomorrow morning. I know we'll have a lot of work to do with some long hours over the next few days. I've got to read this report and figure out what we are going to do."

The young detective and his pretty helper seemed surprised and pleased at the suggestion and nodded their heads in unison.

"And another thing, go have a good meal and bring me the bill in the morning. This is an extraordinary piece of work and you both deserve our thanks. I'll be seeing Collin today before I head home and when he sees this" he tapped their report binder "I'm sure he'll approve my suggestion of a dinner so make sure your waiter hides the bottle of wine so it doesn't show on the bill." Will kept a straight face as he said all this.

Lou could only stammer a surprised thank you and a 'Yes Sir' while Natasha quietly said Thanks, before they quickly turned and left the office, possibly wanting to get away before anything came up to change their good fortune.

Will stood watching them through his office window as they headed across the floor talking and laughing, remembering another time long ago. Smiling, he felt rather pleased with himself, though maybe a little old and maybe a little envious, but still, rather pleased.

Chapter Twenty Six

Will was at his desk by seven-thirty still thumbing through the report which now looked like a chicken with yellow markers tied to its feet had walked all over it for hours. It was not long after Lou and Natasha raced from the building the day before that he left for home and worked into the wee hours of the morning carefully going over their work. When finished, he was even more impressed with their efforts than he had been at first glance. Overlooking no detail and leaving nothing out, they displayed an incredible insight into the thoughts and actions of those being studied. When he finally set the now much marked report down beside his partial bottle of Scotch about four A.M., he knew his two protégés had a secure future in police work.

At ten to eight they were at his door, smiling, happy and ready for work. He motioned them to come in and sit while he sorted out his notes. The silence in the room was comfortable, relaxed.

"Well!" Will said "While you guys were out on the town having a great time at the tax-payers' expense, I was working like the proverbial slave trying to make sense of your report. Actually that wasn't too hard a job. Did you two get out and have a nice meal?"

Lou smiled and shook his head up and down. "It really wasn't at the tax-payers' expense. In fact there is no bill for Collin but it was one of the best meals I've ever had."

"I know I'm getting old and maybe a wee bit daft because I don't understand. What happened?"

Lou looked at Natasha and she smiled and nodded her head in a slight 'yes go ahead' motion.

"Actually Natasha's mother is Italian and taught her all the family's old country cooking secrets. Instead of going out, Natasha came over to my place and whipped up a fabulous spaghetti dinner. And I'll tell you, it was the best I've ever eaten. My contribution was a couple of bottles of Chianti to go along with it. So you see the poor downtrodden citizens are off the hook, this time" and they both laughed, blushing a little.

Will just nodded, smiling, feeling a little like Yente the Matchmaker.

"I guess everyone wins. Collin will breathe a sigh of relief when he hears his entertainment budget dodged a bullet. Now, let's talk about what's to be done."

"Your report is excellent and I've laid out a program based on your assumptions of the value of each suspect. Since your star system gives more stars to those most likely to be our killer, we'll ignore for the moment anyone with less than three stars and concentrate on those with three, four and five."

"There are two things that must be done. Number one above all is Pommeroy and although my instincts say he's not the one, I've been known to be wrong occasionally, so we'll go after him. You two seem to work moderately well together, no fighting I hope, so I want you once more to work together and find out everything you can about him. I want to know his complete history all the way back to grade school. Did he pull wings off flies? Did he ever get drunk as a kid? Did he get speeding tickets? Everything, no detail is too small." Will had a list in front of him and checked off several items.

"How deep should we go?" Lou asked.

"Stop when you hit rock bottom. Go everywhere you can without a court order and if you run into problems, Natasha, you smile, ask nicely and I'm sure you'll get any information you need. Do what is necessary without breaking the law and let everyone know this is a homicide investigation and we won't tolerate any crap. I'm tired of this one and I want it over."

"Job number two is a continued study of all those on the suspect list. While you're waiting on the information on Pommeroy, go back to the others."

Lou and Natasha stood without a word.

"Okay, on your way. Keep in touch and let me know if you need anything or if you find out anything you think I should know in a hurry." They turned and left and Will noticed Lou had a smile on his face that appeared fixed. That must have been one hell of a spaghetti dinner he thought.

In the silence Will reached for the report and picked up the phone. Within a few seconds his call was answered.

"Collin, I need a warrant to search a suspect's home and car in Mississauga. It's a little thin but if our hunch is right it may turn something up. Do you think you can help?" he listened and shook his head as though the speaker could see him.

"Yes, it's Pommeroy. You have all the details in that report I gave you yesterday. There should be enough there to help you" and again he listened.

"Thanks, I'll come by at ten. That should give you time to catch the judge. See you then" and he hung up. He knew forensics could put together a search team in a couple of hours so he set those arrangements to one side of his mind and again looked over the list of suspects. Pommeroy wasn't the only one he wanted a closer look at. Picking the phone up again Will dialed the local branch of the RCMP. He had a few questions for their Organized Crime division about the boys on Railway Street.

Chapter Twenty Seven

Lou slid a sheet of paper across his desk to Natasha. "Take a look at this" he said.

They had been carefully searching their long list of suspects looking for something that might ring a bell. Both were young and naive enough to believe that tough investigations were solved by a magical piece of evidence jumping out of the blue, capable of enabling an arrest before the hour ended. Although real cases in the real world were solved by hard slogging work, piecing together a million bits of evidence, they still searched for magic bullets.

"This girl's got a husband who could be someone worth a hard look" he said as his workmate read over the details on the paper.

"He was busted for common assault several years ago, beat an assault with a weapon a year later but was convicted of assault last year. It looks like he hasn't changed much, but they only gave him probation on that last one. He was also picked up once for drunk and disorderly after his shift in the steel mill, so I'd have to say he has all the necessary credentials. One must wonder how he'd feel if he knew his wife had visited the Imperial Motel a dozen times to do the horizontal tango with our victim."

"I'd have to say he might be a little upset" Natasha smiled across the desk at Lou. "Do you think we should go and have a chat with him or should we see the wife first?"

"I think it should be the wife first. If we talk to him before her we could open a can of worms and the next thing you know he's pounding the daylights out of her and we have black and whites on their lawn. How about you call her at work and we'll have a quiet little chat somewhere out of the way."

"Good plan, I'll call her. Are you going to tell Detective Deas?" she asked.

"Yea, he should know, and he may have a suggestion or two. I'll go and tell him" and he left her to her phone calls.

Lou's stroll along the corridor to his superior's office gave him a chance to think about the night before and the amazing dinner Natasha prepared in his kitchen.

When she started he stood in the doorway with a glass of wine in hand watching her every move as she worked her magic, and he liked what he saw.

Then she asked him to stir the spaghetti sauce as she prepared the ground beef, deftly mixing all kinds of strange things into it from a vast array of small bottles she had brought. Mashing it all in a bowl she then rolled ten individual meatballs, six for him she said, and four for her. With a smile she told him she had brought everything because she knew he would have none of the ingredients she needed.

They laughed often, especially when he bashfully admitted his only pasta cooking experience was making Kraft Dinner from a box and even that was occasionally inedible. This earned him a playful smack on the arm with a large wooden spoon.

By the time the food was on the plates and they were sitting across from each other, they were more than workmates having a meal together. They were good friends who liked each other and both were being careful not to interfere with the good vibes in the room. They finished off their long and delightful evening washing dishes and laughing heartily at each others stories of weird or strange relatives and funny family events each had attended over the years.

Will's door was open when Lou got to it so he tapped on the frame and stepped in to find Collin Fraser standing with some papers in his hand.

"Hi Lou" he said, "got this one solved yet?"

"Just around the corner Sir, it's just around the corner. In fact, we may have a live one here. Alex Vasco, a real thug who seems to like knocking people about. He has a violent record and an eye-popping wife who was regularly doing the 'dirty' with the dearly departed before he departed." He smiled as he handed both Collin and Will copies of his fact sheet.

Collin read the sheet and handed it back. "You may be right. This is one to be followed up. And by the way Lou, you sure are beginning to talk just like him" and he jabbed a finger at the grinning Will sitting behind his desk. "Next you'll be coming in here smelling of cheap pipe tobacco and Scotch" and he left before either one of them could say anything.

"Cheap pipe tobacco my ass. He'd flip if he knew how much that damned stuff cost me."

"What do you think of this one?" Lou asked, tapping the paper.

"Looks promising, how did you come up with it?"

"Natasha found him. She checked all the females on Jefferson's list, where they lived, if they were married and what kind of lifestyle they had. This Vasco's wife is a hairdresser in Ancaster and from her pictures she's a one hundred percent knockout. She's blonde, built like a 'you know what', and not afraid to show her many attributes. She's also the recipient of several glowing editorial comments in Jefferson's computer. She's thirty-three, five foot seven and her husband works at Dominion Foundries and Steel. He's a big drinker, built like a Mack truck, violent as hell, and has a very short fuse."

"Natasha spent some time on the phone and found out he's been thrown out of the Vienna House on Beach Road near the steel mill so many times they've named a section of the sidewalk after him. If he found out Lindsey, his wife, was helping our publisher relax at the no-tell motel, he may have tied one on and set out to give him a beating. It's not unusual."

"Tell your young lady she did some good work and go check it out."

"Consider it done. I'll let you know what's up when we get back" and he too was gone, leaving Will sitting with the search warrant Collin dropped off just as Lou arrived. He felt like he was finally getting somewhere.

Chapter Twenty Eight

Michael Kalishnikoff relaxed in his armchair listening to the phone ringing in his hand. He knew Rosanne moved slowly and he always gave her several more rings than normal when he called. He also knew if she was in the middle of an inspired literary moment she wouldn't answer the phone at all. He smiled as the ring tone stopped and her cultured voice stated that 'This is Rosanne Drew speaking'.

"Hello my dear, how lovely to hear your voice" Michael said in his distinctive Shakespearean stage voice.

"Oh Michael, how nice of you to call, I've been moping about all morning suffering from a seized up brain over a story I'm into and to hear a cheery voice, especially a Montreal cheery voice, is a godsend." She sounded genuinely happy.

"Well I certainly hope I can bring a ray of sunshine into your life to melt that brain freeze and get you on your way."

"It has already started. I feel better already. Now pray tell me, as if I didn't know, what in the world prompts you to call?"

Years before Michael and Rosanne had been a very hot item in both the Toronto and Montreal art circles. They attended the best parties, mixed at the most lavish book launches and supported the most prestigious charitable events. She was stunningly beautiful and sophisticated in a regal, even imperial manner, and he was suave, urbane, and with such good looks most people missed the hint of the devil peeking out. For many years they cut a wide swath through the literary and theatrical world and often visited Europe together for film fests or book fairs. Many wondered why they never married.

When asked once by a close friend, Michael answered 'Because we see each other only at our best, you know. Marriage would certainly ruin that. One must always remember Churchill's words when asked why he and Clementine slept in separate bedrooms. He said that in the morning she wasn't fit to look at, and he wasn't fit to live with. Rosanne and I understand that.'

"You know full well the only reason I'd call was to hear your voice." Michael said.

"Liar" she laughed.

"Oh Rosanne, you stab me to the quick."

"You're calling about our dearly departed and much unloved publisher, aren't you, you little devil."

"Well my dear, the thought had crossed my mind. You do realize that up here in the big city we get very little news of what goes on in Hamilton, if anything ever does go on in Hamilton. I thought you might be able to fill me in on the progress your police are making in apprehending our hero, the killer."

"I knew it. It isn't me you care about" she pouted. "It's those damn dead people. Well anyway, even though I'm hurt I'll tell you all I know" she laughed.

"The police did come and interviewed me, as I knew they would. I mean let's face it, all they had to do was check the bastard's record and the natural suspects are all the authors he's screwed over all these years. I would think their major problem is figuring out which one of us did it. It's going to be fun to see what they come up with. It would probably make a great mystery story. You know, rotten publisher gets murdered and the only suspects are his authors and everyone else in the publishing industry. I've never written a murder mystery but I might when they solve this one."

"I love it" Michael said. "Just make sure I'm in it and don't forget to bring out my sophistication, brilliance and of course my razor sharp wit."

"Ha! That should all take up less than a page" she laughed.

"Enough of this bashing poor Michael, tell me, what's going on in Steel Town?"

"The police have been quite quiet about this one. They held a press conference right after the murder but there hasn't been much since. There have been one or two small items in the paper but I think they've given up on the botched robbery theory because there has been no mention of it."

"Yesterday in an official release, they said the investigation is ongoing and there were still several individuals they wanted to interview in their fact gathering efforts. The usual pap when they don't want to say anything or they have nothing to say but feel they should make some kind of noise."

"They went to see Jan, you know, the travel writer and she called me all worried she may have said too much about what a bastard he was. I told her not to worry, the cops know she was in Egypt and there was no way they can consider her a suspect."

"Not unless she flew fourteen hours to Toronto, drove to Dundas, killed him, drove back to the airport and flew fourteen hours back to Cairo. I'm sure someone would have noticed her missing for over thirty hours, particularly those old fogies she was herding around the pyramids" Michael commented.

Rosanne laughed. "You're right. It would be hard to do without drawing some attention."

"So you guess they've given up on the mugging?"

"The newspaper seems to give that impression. They suggest the investigation is far reaching, even going, get this, all the way to Montreal. I wonder how they discovered that. And one police officer said they were following several different leads and hope an announcement would be made soon. That doesn't sound like they're searching for a dumb robber."

Michael sat for a moment sipping his coffee before replying.

"I'm sure you're right my dear. Something has made them think it wasn't some wandering drug thug, but a person doing a planned killing. Good for them. It restores my faith in your local constabulary. They seem to know what they're doing. Thank you Rosanne, you're such a wealth of information, I don't know what I'd do without you." Michael was enjoying all this.

"You're very welcome. I know I'm no good for anything else but to be a conduit transferring information to you but at least it's something." she whined in her best 'poor me' voice.

"It must be difficult holding the phone to your ear with your wrist firmly stuck to your forehead, my dear." he sympathized.

"Oh shut up, you rotten person you."

"Keep in touch my dear, take notes and get all the gory details. I love to hear your voice, especially when you're reciting facts about Peter's passing. It warms my old heart. Do call and let me know if anything changes, please."

"I will, and you keep safe there with all those beautiful French Canadian girls" and she rang off, chuckling.

The elderly Russian author gently laid the receiver into its cradle and turned back to his keyboard where his next book lay half finished, wondering if the police would ever solve this one.

Chapter Twenty Nine

Natasha's call to Lindsey Vasco was met with a panicky response. It took the policewoman several minutes to talk her down to a reasonable level and get her to agree to a discussion about her extracurricular activities with the publisher. In the end, Natasha simply brought the hammer down and told her she would send a 'black and white' to the hair salon and have a couple uniformed officers bring her down to headquarters, in cuffs if necessary, for a videotaped interview. She explained it would make much more sense for Lindsey to meet them somewhere discreet and out of the way to answer their questions. Mrs. Vasco, scared to death, reluctantly agreed.

On the way to the rendezvous Natasha explained the problem to Lou while he drove.

"You have to understand, she's terrified of her husband. He's working the afternoon shift right now, three pm to eleven pm and won't get home before midnight. She claims he always stops at a beer parlor near the mill for a few and will roll in about twelve-thirty, maybe one o'clock. She doesn't want him to get even a hint of this meeting, so we have to meet at a secluded park. It's the best I could do without spooking her altogether. She's been a naughty girl and she doesn't want her husband to find out."

"The park is fine. We can ask her anything we want within ten minutes and she can be on her way. You did a good job just getting her to agree" Lou said as he swung off Wilson Street and drove down Sulphur Springs Road toward the Hermitage Park, the focal point of a secluded area surrounding the ruins of a huge old burned-out stone mansion. Now run by the local Conservation Authority, it stood roofless with broken walls and glass-less windows, like something from a Jane Austen novel set on the moors of southwest England. Though not very historical, local history buffs had worked hard to garner tons of government money to have the site turned into an area with walking trails, benches and grassy meadows, surrounded by bushes and trees. It was a perfect place for discreet meetings by naughty people, but this time there was only one naughty person involved, Lindsey Vasco.

"There's her car" Natasha pointed to a red Honda sitting alone in a corner of the large tree studded parking lot. "Pull up beside it and she'll jump in." Lou did as directed.

Within moments a very nervous and spectacularly endowed blonde huddled low in the back of the unmarked police car, looking every which way to see who might be around. Both Lou and Natasha marveled at how attractive she was.

"This better be quick. I only get an hour for lunch and it took me ten minutes to get here" the girl said.

"It will be" promised Natasha. "All we need from you is a little information about your relationship with Peter Jefferson and also about your husband's activities several days ago."

"Okay but let's make it quick. What do you want to know?"

Natasha did the questioning. They had decided since Lindsey had first spoken to her, it may be easier to just continue on that way.

"How long have you been involved with Peter Jefferson?"

"Several years I'd say, yea, several years. I met him out at the Rockton World's Fair. It's a one day affair and he had a booth filled with books no one seemed interested in. I stopped and we talked and he was funny, smooth and sexy. I liked him right away."

"Did you know he was married?"

"Sure. He was upfront about it, wore a wedding band, never tried to hide it, and I was the same. He made it clear he wanted some fun if I wanted the same. You know, it just seemed to be good, so we began seeing each other regularly within days." Lindsey had no qualms about her activity with Peter, just a fear of getting caught.

"Do you think your husband had any idea what was going on" Natasha asked.

"Not a chance. If he did, he would have beaten me to a pulp and then thrown me out the front door on my ear. Hell, he might have killed me. He is one of those guys who think it's the woman who makes these things happen and the men are simply innocent bystanders. He's right in some ways I guess. Peter never dragged me into a motel, in fact, I'd call him sometimes and the times he was broke, I'd pay for the room. Like I told you, he was fun and I'm going to miss him." Mrs. Vasco's eyes had a faraway look.

"You said your husband was on afternoons this week" Lou asked this one. "Is that a three to eleven shift?"

"Yes."

"Then he would have been on days last week, a seven to three shift" he probed.

"Normally he would be. The shifts run days, afternoons then nights, but last week he swapped with another guy who needed a week of day shifts, so they traded. The company allows them to do that. They don't care who clocks in as long as it's a warm body that can do the job, so Alex changed his week of days for a week of nights. The guy probably slipped him fifty bucks but I'd never see any of it. He was on the eleven to seven shift all last week and will be next week. Why, do you think my husband had something to do with Peter's murder?" Lindsey Vasco was a little taken aback by the thought.

"Not really" Natasha quickly interjected. "It's just that your name came up in Peter's computer and we have to follow every loose thread we come across. It's all part of the investigation." This seemed to calm her down.

"Are you sure you won't tell my husband about Peter and me?" the blonde beauty asked.

"I see no reason why we would have to involve that part of your life in our reports, but we can't guarantee anything. At the moment, I can say that even if we do talk to Mr. Vasco, the discussion won't have to be about you and Peter. It would be about 'him' and Peter." Lou was firm.

"Okay, and if you need me for anything please call me at the salon. If I'm not there just leave a message, I'll get back to you, I promise. Can I go now?"

"Yes" Natasha said. "Thanks for seeing us and for being so honest and open. It makes our job easier and we appreciate it."

Before she had finished, Lindsey Vasco was out of the car and getting into her own, not caring as she climbed into the small car that her mini-skirt showed a lot more than her long legs. Natasha glanced away from the sight of Lindsey's undergarments to the man beside her, but Lou had the good sense to look down at his papers to check something about two seconds before.

Chapter Thirty

Will left a message on Lou's desk to call when he got back from the meeting with the hair dresser. He wanted Lou available for a meeting with Freddie Trapani at Freddie's home on Railway Street. Although never arrested for anything in his life, many considered Freddie the 'main man' in an organized old style crime family in the area between Niagara Falls and Toronto.

It was unusual for any policeman to be able to arrange an interview with Freddie in just one day; making Will think that 'Freddie the Fox' had something up his sleeve. He wouldn't agree to talk for no reason and Will knew he would need Lou as a backup listener.

"What's up?" Lou asked when he called.

"I've arranged a meet with Freddie the Fox at his home and I thought you'd like to come along and see how the other side lives."

"I'd enjoy that. I've never been in the home of a real live gangster so it might be fun. What time?" Lou asked.

"The appointment is for three. Bring Natasha along with you and bring along your report on the hair dresser you just interviewed. I want some idea on how her husband might fit into all this."

"Okay, I'll get hold of Natasha and we'll have something on paper for you by then."

"Good, be here at two-thirty" and Will hung up.

At two twenty-nine Lou and Natasha stood at Will's door waiting with their report on Lindsey Vasco. Will put some papers away, slipped on his jacket and took the report from Lou's hand. They left the office without a word, Will leading and his two grinning cohorts bringing up the rear.

The house on Railway Street was a tall narrow two and a half story brick built before the First World War. It was during an era of explosive expansion when hordes of European immigrants arrived to work in the factories and steel mills that were built on the south shore of the bay Hamilton sat on. Railroads were being pushed across the land in every direction and Hamilton's industrial base kept growing. During that time, builders were throwing up houses as fast as possible and much like today, they all looked the same. Freddie Trapani's home looked like every other house on Railway Street, only in much better condition.

The three officers climbed the wooden porch steps and as Lou reached for the bell, the door swung open and a man looking like a Sumo wrestler in a Savile Row tailored suit politely asked them to come in.

"You must be the detectives. Come in please, Mr. Trapani is in the library" he said quietly.

Lou stepped aside to let Will lead the way and winked at Natasha, waving her in between them. All three were surprised at the layout.

The interior of the house was original. It was like stepping back a hundred years. The floors were hardwood and perfectly polished, smelling of wax and glistening in the light of the hanging Tiffany lamps. The woodwork of the banister on the stairs as well as the trim around the doors and windows was the original polished oak installed a century ago by craftsmen who took pride in their work. It all sparkled in the soft light.

A wooden coat rack occupied the area by the front door and a shiny old brass shell casing with several umbrellas jutting out, stood beside it. Will half expected a maid to appear in a black outfit with a tiny white lace apron.

"If you follow me, Mr. Trapani is waiting" said the beautifully clad Sumo wrestler led them down the hallway to a closed door. Tapping twice he opened it, standing aside to let them enter. Again, there were more surprises.

Freddie Trapani was about six feet tall, slender and with a head of perfectly groomed white hair that back dropped a strikingly handsome face. Will had never met the man but recognized him immediately from photos he had seen at work over the years. The photos did him no justice because no picture in a police file could convey the style, gravitas and sheer power of the man stepping toward them with his hand extended. He filled the room.

"Welcome gentlemen and you as well young lady" and he turned to Will with a smile saying "how nice of you to bring a beautiful woman with you. It makes life so much more pleasant than just having us old men around."

With a sophistication and genuineness none had expected or encountered before, Freddie took Natasha's hand, raised it to his lips and breathed a kiss onto her fingertips. Even in full uniform with gun on her hip and handcuffs attached to her belt, the girl was a charmed princess standing surprised, a little flustered and not sure of what to do next.

Sensing this, Freddie gently guided her to a chair at his desk and said "You get the best seat in the house Officer, and gentlemen, these are for you" and he pointed to chairs on either side of her. With style and grace Freddie the Fox turned a possible problem into a gentle and comfortable welcome. Knowing all was well, he moved around his desk to slip into his black leather swivel chair and asked "Well lady and gentlemen, what can I do for you?"

His office-den-library spoke of taste, elegance and wealth. On the wall behind the desk hung a large Bateman oil of a deer standing in trees near a meadow. Not a print as most Bateman owners hung in their home, but the original oil that prints are made from. It probably cost as much as Lou's car.

The three other walls of the room were lined with books, many in sets bound in leather but a great number looking old and worn. Will, who loved books more than gold, thought they appeared to be very collectible.

"You have quite a collection of books Mr. Trapani, some appear to be first editions."

"And you have a good eye, Detective Deas. There are over one hundred first editions in this room. All those who know me keep an eye open for anything that might interest me when they travel, so I'm always adding to my collection. You sound like a book lover" and the man reputed to be the head of the Southern Ontario Mob stood, walked to the bookcase on his left, opened a hinged glass cover and gently slipped a thin magazine from its place. Turning, he passed it to Will. It was an old Life Magazine.

"This is one of my most prized possessions. It is a September the first, nineteen fifty two copy of Life Magazine. It contains the first publication of Ernest Hemingway's 'Old Man and The Sea'. A week later, on September the eighth, Scribners released the book and I have a first edition of that as well, but what you're holding is a real treasure. That's a piece of history in your hands."

Will reverently opened the magazine to the marker jutting from the top, in awe of the treasure he held here on Railway Street in the industrial north end of Hamilton Ontario. He was stunned.

"If you like classic books you'll love this" he said as he handed a volume to his appreciative guest.

"This is in Cyrillic script" Will said.

"Right" Freddie grinned. "It's a first edition of Tolstoy's first novel, Childhood."

"It's too bad you can't read it" Will almost whispered.

"Oh but I have. I managed to acquire that book three years ago and decided I must read it. Not a translation but that book. I found a seventy year old retired Russian teacher who taught the language for years. I offered him a substantial hourly rate to teach me to read and understand Russian. I also offered him quite a large bonus, enough to pay for his next car, if he could do it inside eighteen months. Well sir, bonus money is always a great incentive. He came here three times a week and I studied hard and I started slowly on the book fifteen months after I got it and had little trouble reading it cover to cover." Obviously he was proud of his accomplishment.

After carefully examination, Will passed the book and the magazine to his colleagues before reverently handing them back to their owner. Knowing he would seldom have an opportunity like this, he was in no hurry to let it slip away.

"My mother instilled in me the love of reading and a great respect for books" Will said. "She would raise hell if you didn't keep the dust jacket on or if you laid it open face down. I can still hear her sternly telling me to use a bookmark, and if you ever folded a page or the sin of sins, marked a book with a pen, you never heard the end of it." He stopped, thinking of those days.

"It's funny even now I always buy hard cover and if I want or need to make notes, I get a paperback copy and do my marking in the small one" Will said.

Freddie smiled as he put the book back behind the glass and returned to his chair. "Your mother was a woman with great sense. I'm glad it rubbed off on you Detective Deas. Now folks, it's back to more mundane things. What can I do for you?"

"We're here about the recent Peter Jefferson murder and we have to follow up on every piece of information we come across. I thought you may be able to fill in a few blanks for us" Will said to start the interrogation.

"I understand and yes I did hear about the murder. Rather ghastly if you ask me. Uncivilized, is it true he had a pen in his neck and he bled to death?"

"Yes" Will answered, "he was drunk and heading for his car when he was hit."

"Poor man, but at least he didn't get to drive and hurt someone else. Be that as it may, no one deserves to die that way, so tell me Detective, what has all this got to do with me?" Freddie said.

"In the course of our investigation we discovered the victim had some business dealings with you and we're questioning all those with any interaction with him over the past few years. Could you tell us of your dealings with him?"

"I certainly could. Your scrutiny of him would show he, or his company, borrowed a large sum of money from a company I have an interest in and he has been repaying it, somewhat sporadically, over the past few years."

Lou indicated he had a question. "How much did he borrow?"

"I think the original amount was ten or twelve thousand dollars." Freddie said, and then followed his answer with a little background.

"Mr. Jefferson's business had its ups and downs. I guess most do from time to time. During the downs, they often need working capital but in many cases can't get it from conventional sources such as banks, finance companies and mortgage lenders. That's when they turn to companies like mine. We lend money to those who can't get funds anywhere else, and we charge a higher rate of interest for this service. Some look down on what we do, some even call us loan sharks, but believe me, there are many good solid businesses in this city that needed and utilized a service like ours in their early days."

"You say he made his loan payments, let's see, the word you used was sporadically. What do you mean by that?" Lou asked.

Freddie spread his hands open, palms up in the age old 'who knows' gesture. "He would go three months just fine then I guess run into a rough spot and need some prodding to get in with some money, that sort of thing. A lot of our clients are like that, needing a phone call or two as a prompt to get in with some money. He did pay, mind you, but he could be a pain in the ass. Oh, I'm sorry" he said to Natasha.

"No problem sir" she smiled. "In our line of work we sometimes are exposed too much stronger language than that."

"I guess you do but I still believe in my father's advice. He always said to never swear before ladies, always let them swear first" again the charming smile as he looked at Natasha.

"Damn good advice too sir, your father sounds like one hell of a man." and all had a good laugh over her handling of his apology.

Lou stepped in again. "Then you know of no reason why someone would want him dead?"

"No one who runs a legitimate business would want to see that happen to a client who owes the business money and is paying, even sporadically. Repayment is the foundation of our business. We keep good books. We report our profits to the government and we pay taxes on those profits. If someone is going around killing our clients, we would soon be out of business. No sir, I hope you find out who did this and put him away for a long time." Freddie the Fox was the epitome of good business sense.

"So there's little chance someone in your organization might have made a mistake, lost their temper while trying to collect an overdue payment" Will asked.

"I would be very angry if one of my employees did something as stupid as that. I know there still lingers the impression that Italians and illicit activities go hand in hand, but that was a long time ago. We are businessmen now. Mind you, there are some dishonest Italian businessmen just as there are some dishonest Scottish businessmen, but the vast majority are hard-working and law abiding. No, Detective Deas, we may be tough and we don't like someone treating us badly, but no one carries a gun anymore. It's much easier to keep a stable of good lawyers on call and sue people when you have a problem."

He sat quietly looking at them and when no more questions came his way he stood to signal the meeting was over and moved around the desk to stand in front of Natasha.

"You haven't had any questions, young lady. Is there anything you would like to ask me?"

Taken aback, Natasha recovered quickly and said "Yes, there is. Where were you educated?"

"I graduated from McMaster University many years ago and went on to Harvard where I received my law degree. From there I went to Cambridge in England for a year to study the humanities. I was lucky in that my parents believe a good education is necessary for a good life and they had the money from their vending machine business to pay for one. I have been quite lucky."

She held out her hand to him. "It has been a pleasure meeting you and seeing your beautiful home. Thank you."

"Well thank you for brightening it up for a few moments" and he moved to open the door they had entered by. "Vince will show you out and if there is anything else just phone. I'll get back to you as quickly as possible" and he closed the office door leaving them in the care of the wrestler in his thirty-five hundred dollar suit.

On the way back to the station Will asked Lou and Natasha what they thought of Freddie the Fox and if they had an opinion on his involvement. Their response was as he expected.

Lou spoke first "He's not a player in this one. I believe him when he says it would be bad business to whack a client who owes you money, especially money you have declared and are paying tax on.

"I agree with Lou" his pretty co-worker said. "My mother told me a long time ago the Italians don't kill their clients anymore. She said maybe they might get a little upset with a partner or boss who was getting uppity and decide some discipline was in order but customers no, that went out of style many years ago.

Lou turned to her with an amazed look on his face "are you kidding me? When the hell would your mother say that?"

"When I talked to her about joining the police force I asked if she thought my Italian last name would cause any problems. We had a long discussion about it. My mom is pretty wise, you know."

"Your mom is very wise" Will told her "and it will do you well to keep her words in mind. She's right about organized crime. Even in the Godfather, which some suggest was as close to a mob documentary as you could get, they only killed their own. Sonny, Fredo, Moe Greene, Luco Brazzi were all part of the organization. I agree with you, Freddie the Fox had nothing to do with this."

They drove in silence for several minutes before Will asked about the Vasco lady.

"What about this hair dresser's husband? Do you guys think he's a prospect?"

"I do" Natasha said.

"What about you Lou?"

"I don't know. Natasha thinks a husband who finds his wife getting it on with some guy is a suspect but he was working so I have a lot of misgivings."

"Well, check it out. Check the steel mill, see if he was really working, she could be lying. You two take care of that for me."

Lou looked at Natasha and had difficulty hiding his smile. She had the same problem.

Chapter Thirty One

Will sat at his desk for the rest of the afternoon with the door closed and the phone on mute. He had a lot of thinking to do and he wanted no interruptions.

This case, which should have been easy to solve, was turning into a stinker. Usually the problem was finding someone who wanted the victim dead and once you had done that, the rest would fall into place. With research and questioning he knew the suspect would stumble, make a mistake or change their story somehow. Very few people could fabricate a story and remember every detail through several questionings by skilled investigators.

This one was different. With an overabundance of people happy that Peter was dead, how did you choose which one of the cheery group to zero in on. Several of them had very good reason to want him dead and some had the opportunity and ability. The problem was that none had given him reason enough for a video-taped interview in an interrogation room in the station. Will knew he was missing something and the best way to find out what, was to go back to the beginning and start all over again. That would mean another visit with Mrs. Jefferson.

He called Lou and told him to round up his notes on the last meeting with the widow, and then phoned her to make an appointment for another interview.

At four-thirty Mrs. Jefferson welcomed Will and Lou at a newly repaired screen door and ushered them into her home. She looked years younger than the lady who greeted them a week before and she wasn't the only thing in make-over mode. The home was getting its share of attention as well.

The widow's hair had been cut in a page-boy style that was quite attractive. She wore more makeup than he remembered from his last visit, and it looked professionally applied. Her expensive looking jeans fit snugly from her new pumps up to her well-shaped backside. The V cut in her black cotton T shirt swept quite low and it too was snug. The widow Jefferson had morphed into a very different woman from the grieving Mrs. Jefferson.

"Please excuse the mess" she said, waving them into the newly painted living room. "I'm having a little work done and I'm afraid it will be like this for a few more days."

"No problem" Will said, little bells ringing in his head.

The old beat up sofa was gone as were the chairs, faded drapes and bent curtain rod. The kitchen table had been moved into the living room and placed in front of the fireplace, so they pulled up chairs and sat down.

"They're tiling the kitchen floor tomorrow morning so, this room is where everything has to go. I hope this is all right with you" she smiled.

"It's no trouble at all, we're sorry to bother you. It's just that we have a few more questions before we wrap this thing up and we thought you might be able to help" Will said, smiling as well.

"Ask away then. The workers have finished for the day and we'll have some peace and quiet, if not order."

Lou said thanks and asked the first question.

"You said the last time we were here that your husband came home the evening he was killed, had supper, watched Jeopardy with you and then went out to the bar. Is that correct?"

"I think it is. Peter never had a normal everyday schedule like most people and he came and went quite irregularly, so I could have been wrong. I was very upset when you spoke to me you know, I could have been wrong." She sat twisting a handkerchief in her hands.

"I think you may have been" said Will. "Bar staff said he had been there drinking continuously from about five pm until he left through the back door after twelve-thirty. Can you comment on those details?"

"I could have been wrong. After all, you were here shortly after my husband was murdered. I was still in shock. I could have been wrong."

"Well, was he in the habit of not coming home for dinner and sitting in a bar 'till closing time. Did he do this sort of thing often?" Will pressed her.

"Oh there were times when he was under pressure he would drink too much and forget about coming home or calling. That's probably what happened the evening he died. I can't recall."

"But did he do this sort of thing often?" Will asked.

"What do you mean by often?"

"Did he do this once a week, or twice a week, or less than once a week?" Will didn't try to hide his annoyance.

"Only about once a week" she almost whispered.

Will nodded, knowing she was not being totally truthful because the bar where he was killed and the Press Club both verified Peter Jefferson did this more than just once a week.

Will put a small asterisk beside his note about her insistence she could have been wrong about her husband coming home for an evening meal. Was her acknowledgment of her husbands drinking habits a deliberate lie or was it a wife's natural instinct to protect the memory of her man. He jotted down a few more notes and then moved on.

"You also said the business was very bad and had been for some time. Did Mr. Jefferson have a life insurance policy when he died?"

"Oh you mean all these repairs and the work going on in the house? No, Peter had no life insurance. This is all being covered by my parents. My dad came around and suggested we get a smaller home and said we couldn't sell this one because of the condition it was in. He offered to pay for the fix-up if he got his money back when it sold. I agreed."

At that moment the front door swung open with a bang and Mrs. Jefferson's seventeen year old son stomped in.

"Hi mom" he hollered as he made his way through tools and boxes of tiles en route to the refrigerator. "Anybody call for me?"

"No dear. No one called." She smiled and shook her head.

"Okay, if it rings I'll get it in my room" he shouted as he headed for the stairs, glass of milk and chunk of something in his hand.

"Oh and by the way" he called from the stairs. "I took those papers to the bank and arranged the transfer of the US funds into your account. The bank said it would all be done today" and he disappeared up the stairs to his room.

Mrs. Jefferson turned to the two detectives and smiled warmly. "He's been such a pillar of strength since his dad passed. He runs errands, does banking, cleans up after himself and keeps an eye on his sister. I would not have believed it possible. Like today, his dad had a large amount of US money stashed away for a rainy day and my son took care of the details involved in transferring it into our account. He really has been wonderful." Again she shook her head.

"One last thing" Will gently shifted back to his questions. "Can you remember your husband having a major argument with any of his authors in the weeks before the tragedy?"

"Not anything out of the ordinary, no, nothing unusual. There was always some shouting, arguing about deadlines, advance money or marketing but these things were routine."

"Did he have bad relations with any particular writer more than the others" Will probed?

"Not really. He certainly didn't get along with that Drew lady, the old crude woman from the east end of the city. She could be quite rude. If I answered the phone when she called, she always asked for Peter using a vulgar expression. It's no wonder he always ended up screaming at her. Other than her, no, I wouldn't say one was worse than another."

"I have a final question as well" Lou said. "What are your plans after all this is done" and he waved his hand, indicating the repairs and renovations.

"The children and I have already discussed that and after the house is sold we're going to move out of the area and start anew. We all have some bad memories of our life here and although Peter's death was a tragic occurrence, it does give us a chance for a fresh start."

Will flipped his notebook shut and motioned to Lou. "Thank you Mrs. Jefferson, you've been a big help and I'll get back to you. Now Detective Shatz and I will be on our way" and he stood, shook her extended hand and followed her to the door.

Once in the car Will turned to Lou and asked one question and made one observation. The question was "How did she know about the US funds in the bank account that was hidden in his private section of his computer?"

The observation was "did you get the impression that she was not unhappy at this chance for a new beginning, a new life?" Lou said nothing.

It was a very quiet ride back to the station.

Chapter Thirty Two

The search warrant for the Mississauga writer's place proved to be a dud. They had contacted the Peel Regional Police and after meeting with the head of their forensic unit, the officers from both forces descended on Albert Pommeroy's condo. It didn't take long for them to determine he was not their man. He may have hated his publisher, and could justify his feeling, but when they were done searching his car and going over his apartment, they had no evidence the chain smoking tough talking mystery writer was implicated.

Both Will and Lou worked the time line and agreed Pommeroy could have done it. He had no clear alibi for his time between eleven pm and five am, and had ample time to drive from his home to the bar, do the deed and drive back home. Their problem was that there wasn't a shred of evidence to prove that's what he did and he was an innocent man until they could prove he wasn't.

The parking garage at his condo building had no camera and kept no records, electronic or video, that might prove he left and drove anywhere that evening. The one camera behind the bar was aimed at the back door and had a brief image of the victim leaving. It was no help at all. The forensic searchers that examined his car found nothing. No blood anywhere that he may have brought into the car on his hands or shoes and no wood fibers, nor anything flat that could be used as a weapon. None of the items taken from the victim were found. They had nothing other than their suspicions and the author's obvious and self-confessed hatred of the publisher. In a court of law you can't convict on suspicions.

To cap it, their discussions with Pommeroy's brother indicated the writer was in a normal mood when they met to go to the airport. In his words, Al was the same old surly Al as they checked in, and if anyone would notice a difference, it would be him.

Will and Lou tossed it back and forth on the way back to Central and came to the same conclusion. Pommeroy, for all his tough talk and bravado had too much to lose from Jefferson's death, and he was not their killer in this case.

As they drove along Will sat staring blankly out the windshield for a long time and finally turned to Lou and asked "Lou, tell me, why do people kill?"

"What do you mean, why do people kill? Hell, there are more reasons for people to kill someone than you can shake a stick at. It would take all day to list them all."

"Then list some" Will asked.

"Vengeance, there's one. Money, boy, that's got to be a main one. How about infidelity? One hell of a lot of people have met their end because they were being naughty and got caught. There's passion, rage, losing control, they would have to be on the list. Accident is another. Sometimes people want to hurt or scare but not kill and end up going a little too far. Another is thrill killing, like Bernardo and that nut case he was bedding. I'd think you'd also have to include self-preservation in the list. There are all kinds of reasons."

"Not really, you listed maybe seven or eight. There's almost none other than those you mentioned. Unless you're very strange, like a contract killer who does it for pay, or one of those nut case serial killers who prey on hookers, there are very few reasons people kill others deliberately. Accidentally yes, it often happens, but deliberately, not so much." Will went silent again, thinking, staring out at the road then turned back to Lou.

"Did you notice when you listed your reasons you never mentioned hate. You never said a person killed because they hated someone. Lou, I think we've been running at this the wrong way. We went for the most obvious motive."

"We've been running around trying to figure out who hated him the most. We've been wondering what person, or more likely, which author hated Jefferson enough to kill him. I think the person who killed him didn't do it because he or she hated Peter Jefferson, they killed him for one of those reasons you listed."

Lou said nothing. He had seen Will like this before, speaking more out loud to himself than to his partner beside him. He was fitting the pieces together and

Lou didn't want to intrude and break Will's train of thought. He knew the best thing to do was to keep quiet, drive, and wait.

Will sat silent for several more minutes and finally spoke.

"Lou, I think we'll take some time this afternoon to work this out. When we get back to the station I'm going home. I want you to gather up all your notes and files on this case, find Natasha and tell her to bring everything she has, and both of you come up to the house. We're going to have a long session on this, and we might as well be comfortable. You two are both kind of bright and we'll see what the three of us can do if we give it a real workout" and he slid back into his quiet thinking mode for the rest of the journey.

Chapter Thirty Three

By the time Natasha and Lou arrived at the house Will had changed into jeans, poured a drink, lit his pipe and carried his cat out to a group of chairs around a table beside the pool. He looked more like a businessman planning the acquisition of his next company than a police officer trying to find a killer.

"Do we just walk in?" Natasha asked as they walked up the driveway past Will's car.

"No, he'll be out by the pool so we take the path to our right and stroll into his garden" and Lou guided her toward the narrow path.

"Hi guys, grab a chair or lounge and have a seat" Will called, waving them over. Natasha had never been to Will's home and now knew why he spent so much time there.

The house was a 1960's style two story, four bedroom brick with an attached double garage. When built it was considered an expensive home for an upscale market and sat on a lot considered by present day standards to be huge.

Across the back of his home Will had put in a concrete patio. It separated the house from the sparkling twenty by forty foot pool they were now sitting beside. Around them, everywhere she looked, Natasha saw bushes, trees and beautifully manicured lawns bordered by flowers and large, carefully placed stones. She felt as though she was sitting on an estate in the country, not in a city subdivision surrounded by other houses. The feeling of privacy was complete. Natasha was enchanted, and she looked upon her superior with a new respect.

"You like?" Will asked.

"I love it. It's so quiet and peaceful. Now I know why you come back home whenever you need to think. Lou didn't tell me it was so lovely. Do you maintain it yourself?" She sparkled like the pool.

"Oh indeed I do. I get down on me hands and knees in the dirt with me wee plants lassie. That way I've no need of one of those therapists the brass are always trying to push on you after a really bad case."

Lou came out the back door of the house with two drinks and handed one to Natasha before pulling up a seat beside her.

"It was gin and orange, wasn't it?" he asked as she sipped.

"It's perfect" she smiled, patting his hand, causing Will to grin and think that if Lou was remembering what she drank, he was hooked.

"I was just telling Will how much I loved his place. It's so beautiful and so quiet."

"It is that. I've learned from Will that one needs a sanctuary in this job and it works, doesn't it Will? We've come up with some good solutions in some tough cases sitting out here sipping a cool one."

"That we have laddie and that's what we're going to do today. The three of us are going to solve this one before you leave tonight. I hope pizza and wings will do for dinner, along with a nice Chianti of course."

"Sounds great and since I'm new and you guys have been through this before, why don't I just listen, take notes and get a feel of things" Natasha said, opening a small folio to get a notepad and pen.

"Okay, but jump in when you feel like it. I know you have a brain in that head and I'm sure you can contribute, so join in" Will said as he pushed the cat from his lap and picked up his notes.

For the next four hours the three of them tossed ideas around, argued, laughed and slowly worked their way through the original list of suspects not noticing the sun had set and it was getting dark.

By eight-thirty the mosquitoes forced them to move inside where they huddled over papers, a bowl of chicken bones and half eaten pieces of pizza spread across the dining room table. Behind them, on the kitchen counter, lay assorted empty pizza boxes and Styrofoam chicken wing containers. Brainstorming hadn't stopped while the food was consumed.

Outside, Natasha had sat and listened for ten or fifteen minutes before hearing something that prompted her to jump in with an observation. From that point on she was as deeply involved in the discussion as her two fellow officers. It was a good session and brought out things one would notice but the others might miss.

Lou said what convinced him Pommeroy didn't do it was his arrogant conviction that he would win the case against the publisher. He believed the writer wouldn't kill someone he was going to beat anyway, and if he read Pommeroy correctly, the nasty writer would enjoy crowing about his victory everywhere he went.

"The jerk would probably take out an ad in the Spectator to sound off about how he whipped the man who had wronged him."

Will wasn't so sure and asked Natasha to start a file and call it 'possible but not likely'. She placed it on top of the 'not a chance' file which contained details of Jan Henning, whom they had all agreed at the start, was not the killer.

They tossed about the elderly Russian cookbook writer but finally agreed he couldn't be their main man either. The same went for Rosanne Drew and Sonya Franks, two elegant ladies who, if they had truly wanted to kill Peter, would have been more likely to use poison. The stack of possible bad guys was getting smaller.

As they moved through the rest, discarding each as a credible suspect, the discussion between Will and Lou about why people commit murder was raised often. Natasha wanted to know the story and Lou explained about how few reasons there were. She caught on quickly, laughing, saying she always considered infidelity the best reason of all for killing someone, and ordinary hatred to be the worst.

"That's why I've felt from the start that Alex Vasco is a prime suspect. I think he found out about his wife and Jefferson and set about to settle the score. Most men, and especially a thug like Vasco, tend to get a little crazy when thinking about their wife rolling around a bed in a cheap motel with some other guy."

Lou smiled over at her and said "under any other circumstances I'd have to say you're right, but Vasco was working that night. We've checked his time-card and questioned his supervisor. There is no question he punched in about eleven and punched out a little after seven. He was at work that night."

"The time card doesn't mean anything" Natasha said. "My oldest brother has worked in that mill for ten years as a doorman in the soaking pits, at the south end of the rolling mill running along Ottawa Street, the same area Vasco works. Those guys walk in and out of that place like it was a country club. When a stag was held for my brother before his wedding he was doing the three to eleven. About seven he gave his card to a buddy and left for the stag. If you're smart and you've been in the mill any length of time, you have a buddy you can trust. My brother's buddy punched him out and put his time card in the appropriate place."

Will slowly turned from Lou and looked at her. "Can we check that out?"

"I don't see how. If an employee is caught punching some other card they get fired, and so does the guy whose card was punched! No one will ever admit they've ever punched some other person's card at shift's end."

"So you mean to say that a worker could walk out of that place and disappear for a few hours or the whole shift and no one would notice?" Will asked.

"Only certain workers on certain jobs could leave unnoticed. The man operating the two-high rolling mill couldn't, if he did the whole place would shut down. The guy running the coiler couldn't because the steel would crash into his machine and again, the place would shut down. But there are others all over the place, burners, slingers and guys like that who wander in and out, sleep for hours, go over to Tim Horton's for coffee and donuts, nobody checks."

"How do you know all this stuff?" Lou asked her.

She grinned. "I worked three summers there when I attended McMaster. My brother got me a job as a coil marker. When they wound up a strip of steel into a coil, someone had to write the heat number on it, that's what they call a group of ingots sent to the rolling mills, a heat. I had to mark the gauge, width and several other details on the hot coil with a three foot long stick with a large piece of special white chalk attached to the end. That was my job. I wore a long silver insulated coat and apron, plus a mask for protection because the coils were still hot enough to start a fire when I wrote the numbers on them. It was hot work but it was fun and the money was great."

Lou shook his head. "You must have had a tough time fighting off all those macho steel workers."

"No such luck. My brother insisted my shift be the same as his, and considering his size and his Italian last name, believe me, there were few passes made."

"I'll be damned" said Will and shook his head in wonder. "It's amazing what you learn at these kinds of sessions. Maybe we better take another look at Alex Vasco. Lou, invite him down to the office and you and Natasha ask him a few questions. With her knowledge of the modern steel mill operation, he'll have more trouble fooling her than me."

"I'll get on to it in the morning."

"Good, I think Natasha is right about infidelity being a major reason for murder and we'll have to tread lightly here. Be careful with him and don't bring his wife into it unless you really have to. Get his car details and tell him a car like his, with the same last three plate numbers was parked outside a bar where a crime had taken place. Con him, see how he reacts and then let me know" and Will stood and stretched.

"We've done enough tonight. It's been a good session. Lou, thanks for all the effort and Natasha, you were great. You have a real future in this kind of work. Now let's call it a day and meet at the station tomorrow morning. We have a murder to solve.

Chapter Thirty Four

Will considered Natasha's observations about infidelity. He thought about the many terrible things it had caused people to do, and the many tragedies he had seen over the years because of it. Her comments and how she felt about this case proved that she was quite a girl and fast becoming quite a cop.

Lou left with her, the two strolling down Will's driveway hand in hand, unaware the old detective was watching them through the window of his darkened living room. Will thought they made a cute couple. Much like he and his wife were a cute couple back in the days before he became a cop and she didn't have to play second fiddle to every villain in the city. He shrugged, sighing audibly, knowing that was then and this was now and there was nothing he could do to change what had passed.

He stood many minutes at the window, long after their car had pulled away from the curb, sipping his Scotch and thinking of Peter Jefferson's body spread out in the alley with a cheap fountain pen jutting from his neck. Natasha was right. This was indeed a crime of passion, and that meant there were only two real suspects. Number one was Alex Vasco, and number two was Mrs. Jefferson.

Will finally moved away from the window and back through the quiet house to start cleaning up. His mind worked well doing labor requiring little thought and as he picked up empty pizza boxes he considered all the possibilities from their discussion.

Now convinced it was a crime of passion, he mentally eliminated all of the writers as possible suspects. If any one of them wanted Peter dead they would do what most people do who have a festering long time hate. They would explode one day, go postal, blowing away the object of their hate with a shotgun, or bashing their head in with a hammer. This was not that kind of case. This was a carefully planned incident by someone who knew the victim well.

Will finished loading the dishwasher and returned to the dining room table to sort through the papers strewn about. He thought about Alex Vasco and how much time he would need to walk to his car in the employee parking lot, drive to the bar and confront Peter Jefferson about his wife. Will knew how the drunk would react, laughing at the outraged husband, telling him to buzz off and dismissively turning toward his car. One could understand a man like Vasco lashing out in a blind rage, knocking him to the ground unconscious with one blow to the back of Jefferson's head. He may have even had a flat piece of steel from the mill with him to use as a weapon, a piece he could take back to work and toss into a scrap bin.

Will could imagine the gruff steelworker standing over the man who played fast and loose with his wife and he could see him reach down to pick up a pen that had fallen from the bastard's pocket and knew he would look at it with curiosity.

It would be at this time Jefferson would start to regain some semblance of consciousness and possibly start to yell. Vasco would panic, bend down to shut his victim up and in a blinding second, deal the blow with the pen that would end Peter Jefferson's life.

Knowing what he had done, Alex Vasco would then empty all of the dead man's pockets to make it look like a robbery, run to his car and drive back to work. The whole affair would require him to be away from the mill for two, maybe three hours.

Will also thought about Mrs. Jefferson. She sure didn't seem like a murderer, but then neither did Karla Homolka or Lizzie Borden or Bonnie Parker. Killers came in many different shapes and sizes.

Will wondered what a woman would do if she found out her husband was leading a completely different life away from home and spending money on other women while she and her children did without. He was damned sure a lot of ordinary women would be capable of murder if they stumbled onto a secret section of their husband's computer revealing this type of activity. Hell he thought, finding that information, and then killing her husband would almost constitute justifiable homicide.

He sat a long time going over each detail, sorting facts tossed about during the evening's session. He knew there was something he had missed but it was late and he was tired. He knew there was something he had heard that would help but it wouldn't come to him, so he shrugged, locked the doors, turned out the lights and went to bed.

Chapter Thirty Five

Will spent the morning in his office shuffling papers while waiting for Lou and Natasha to return from their questioning of Alex Vasco. They decided not to bring him into the station from his home in Stoney Creek, figuring since it was just a preliminary interview, there was no need to set off alarms should it turn out to be a dead end.

Lindsey, the wayward wife, was working that morning and Alex would be preparing for his three to eleven shift, so Lou drove with Natasha to conduct the interview. Both he and his partner were surprised at how well the questioning went.

Vasco bought the story of the license plate number and seemed happy to co-operate with the two officers visiting him, especially the pretty one with the cute blonde pony tail.

He had clocked in on the night in question just before eleven and claimed to have been in the mill all night. He said his car never left the employee parking lot and suggested the witness who gave the police the information about the car must have got the plate number or the make and model wrong.

He remembered the night because it had been a bad one for him, a torch man in the rolling mill. Officially his job title was Burner, and he could wield a three foot long acetylene torch much the way the Three Musketeers used their swords. He explained how his main job was to cut test samples of 'skelp' steel, the type used for heavy pipe. He explained how he would cut a two to three inch piece of steel from the strip and place it in a shear for cutting. Inspectors would then inspect the cut piece, decide whether it was good or bad and make a report. The piece he cut was then tossed into a scrap bin.

His secondary job was to be available whenever an emergency required a burner, and that night he was needed almost from the moment he stepped into the building.

They had changed rolls on the main rolling mill and the first couple of ingots run through the mill for reduction into a long coil of steel would have a cold leading edge. This was caused because the giant rolls in the mill were still cold from the change. This always caused problems and as often happened, when the leading edge of the speeding strip of steel came down from those cold rolls they would start to bounce and lift off the conveyors, ending like an accordion wrapped around walkways, rolling platforms and catwalks. They needed Burners to quickly cut away all the scrap spread throughout the place because another strip was on its way from the main mill and it would crash into the first one piled up on the conveyors. Alex Vasco had his work cut out for him that evening and his bosses would be able to testify to his constant presence. He smiled and said he was sorry but he couldn't have seen the robbery they were investigating.

Lou's notes were extensive and a quick check of the steel mills operations verified Alex Vasco's story. Not only was he there, it had been a bad night and he had worked like hell, punching out at seven twelve in the morning. As an afterthought Lou asked the super to fax him a copy of the mill's internal operations report for that night.

The two walked into Will's office about one thirty and gave him all the details. On the drive back to the station they had discussed Alex Vasco's story and how after checking some details, all seemed in order. Lou accepted the story but still had some misgivings.

Their report to Will was that Vasco was not their man but Lou still had a few minor things to check out, and his boss said sure, go for it.

Will sat silently for several minutes thumbing through their notes then asked the two a simple question.

"Why do you guys think someone killed Peter Jefferson?"

Lou answered first "Because he was a bastard and everyone hated him."

"I don't think so" Natasha said, putting a hand on Lou's arm. "I think he was killed because he was screwing around with too many married women and someone went after him."

"Then it wasn't an author. He was done in by an irate husband."

"Right" Natasha said.

"Then Lou might be right in his misgivings about Vasco. What do you think about that Lou?"

"It does make some sense. None of the authors seem like prime suspects with the exception of Pommeroy. Three of them were out of town, a couple were either too old or too far away to have done it, so maybe Natasha's right. Vasco has a pretty good alibi and if it stands up to close scrutiny maybe we should go back over the list of playthings in the computer and find out if there's another husband out there capable. Maybe we missed something."

"Alright then, I have another question. Did either of you tell Mrs. Jefferson about the US bank account her husband had hidden?"

Both of them shook their heads no as though tied together with rope.

"Neither of us had a chance. You sent us out to see Lindsey Vasco. We did the check on Jennifer North, the writer in Calgary, and we talked to the Jamaican Police about Winston and got an all clear on him. No, you would have known if we had talked to her." Lou was emphatic.

"Then how did she know Jefferson had a stash of US dollars?" Will asked.

"He probably told her." chipped in Natasha "Husbands have been known to set aside something for their family in case of emergency you know."

"That would be out of character for our victim" Will said. "Think about this. If she by some chance got into his computer and found out about his hidden US funds, maybe she also found out about his girlfriends, jewelry purchases and everything else he had hidden there. How would she react?"

"Not too well" Lou said.

"Hell, if it was me, I'd kill him!" Natasha spat.

"Exactly, that would be any wife's reaction. Here she's living in a rundown house filled with beat-up furniture, wearing worn out clothes and struggling to get by, while he's out spending all kinds of dough on his playmates. I think we may have been looking in the wrong place. We have a golden prospect in Mrs. Jefferson. If she knew what was going on, I think she would be more than a little miffed."

"She seems less like a killer than I do" Natasha said quietly.

"Lou, I think you should call her and then the two of you hop in your car and go pick up the widow Jefferson and bring her in for a conversation. She has some explaining to do and I want her to do it here, on our grounds, and I want it video-taped."

"After you bring her in I'll question her with Collin looking in. While I'm with her I want you two to go back over everything you have about Vasco and make sure there are no holes in his alibi. Now let's get going."

The meeting was over and the two young detectives gathered up their papers and left to call the lady in Dundas. Will had the feeling they were getting very close.

Chapter Thirty Six

Mrs. Jefferson was nervous when she arrived at the station but said nothing until seated at a table across from Will in the barren interrogation room. A tall uniformed officer stood at the door and on the table between them was a small device with a tiny red light. Will reached to the device, pressed a button and the red light gave way to a green one. Will began to speak, stating his name, Mrs. Jefferson's name, the time, the date and a file number. He then looked up and said "What we say and do during this interview will be recorded, do you have any objections to that?"

"I have no objections, I would just like to know what this is all about" and she looked about the room with distaste.

"It's about the death of your husband, Mrs. Jefferson. There are several things we need to get clear in order to wrap up this case."

"Am I a suspect, or under arrest?"

"At the moment we just want to get some answers. You were informed by Officer Schatz that you could have an attorney present but he informed me you felt that unnecessary. You are entitled to have one with you if you want. Do you still feel that you don't want one?"

"Since I have done nothing wrong, I see no need for a lawyer, so I suggest you ask away and I'll answer as best I can and we can get this nonsense over. I have nothing to hide and think it would have saved a lot of time, and been much more comfortable to have done this in my home."

Will asked if she wanted something to drink and she asked for tea. The officer at the door opened it and asked another officer to fetch some. Standing next to that officer was Collin Fraser, watching the interview on closed circuit TV. The pot of tea and a mug were brought to the room almost immediately and Will waited while she poured.

"Do you have a computer?" Will started.

"I do. It's a new one. My old one crashed some time ago and Peter got me a new one" she answered.

"Would you consider yourself computer literate, you know, good at them?" asked Will.

"Heavens no, I do e-mails, look up recipes on that Google thing my son taught me to use, keep a list of names and addresses we use for Christmas cards, that sort of thing, but I'm lost if I have to go beyond that. I never used one before Peter gave me his old laptop a few years ago when he got a new one. Mind you, most of his work was done on his desktop so when mine crashed and died recently he lent me his laptop for a couple weeks while he got me a replacement."

"So you used his new personal unit for a few weeks, the one we found in his car and still have here at headquarters?" Will asked.

"Yes."

"Did your children use it during that period?"

"Leonard and Eleanor? sure, they were on it every minute I wasn't. They were always fighting over who got to use it and who was on it the most time, you know, typical kid stuff. Facebook, they're always onto Facebook you know. They drove me nuts."

"Does Leonard know much about computers?' was Will's next question.

"My son? Oh my God yes, he's a whiz. Peter would call him every five minutes for help with website problems or troubles with a program. Leonard has friends from school, even teachers, who call him with problems. Leonard was always able to find some solution or fix any problem. He would search for something called a free ware or free thing and his solutions seldom cost anything. Yes sir, Leonard is very good at computers" she said with pride.

Collin, standing in the room next door turned from the monitor to a great hulking man beside him and quietly asked "do you think she got into that secret part of the laptop and saw what he was up to Chief?"

Collin's superior thought for a moment before answering.

"Anything's possible but if what she said about her tech skills is half true, I don't think she would have possibly done it herself. Hell, it was beyond all the staff in this place so I'm sure it would take a young, what do you call them, 'a Geek' to open that section. She might have seen it. The problem is proof. You know the prosecutor can't prove which individual did what on a computer. You can often tell if something is done but if four different people are using it unsupervised and as long as the passwords are intact, you can't determine whose fingers touch the keys. I think we have a very real problem with that."

Collin nodded "we talked with the people at the O.P.P. and they said there was no keystroke tracking software on the computer and never had been so we may never know who knew what. It could have been her, or more probably Leonard, but we'll never know" and he turned back to the questioning.

"When did you learn about your husband's US bank account?"

"Oh months ago. Peter told me about it, not the amount mind you, that surprised me, but the account, the bank and the branch. He said if I ever had any problems and he wasn't around to help, I should just go to the bank and get some out."

"Was your name on the account Mrs. Jefferson?"

"No, but he gave me two signed checks I was to keep safely hidden until I needed them. He had worked this out long ago and there was no problem." Mrs. Jefferson was composed, calm.

"Is that what Leonard used to transfer the money he was speaking of when he came home?"

"No, I believe he just took in a copy of the death certificate and the will which left everything to me and the bank did the rest. I left it up to Leonard and he was so helpful."

"Where are the checks signed by your husband?" Will probed.

"I put them through the shredder and they went out with all the other recyclables last week. They were of no more use and one shouldn't leave things like that lying around." She looked straight into Will's eyes as she said this.

"You told us your husband came home for supper that night when he actually had not. Have you had any chance to reconsider the events of that evening?"

"Well I did think about it and I was mistaken. He was a man of action and whims and if he had any schedule, it was erratic at best, so evenings tend to blend together unless there is something special about them. He didn't come home that night and I just shrugged it off. The children and I ate without him. Eleanor went down the street for a sleepover at a friend's house and my son went out after Jeopardy. He's a fan of the show like his mom and dad. After Jeopardy he went to a concert or something in Toronto and didn't come home until quite late, probably about two."

"So you were wrong about your husband coming home that night" Will asked again.

"Yes I was wrong. It was a very difficult time and I guess I wasn't thinking properly. I'm sorry if that caused you any problems."

Outside the Chief turned to Collin, asking him what he thought.

"It's a good story and would make her look honest and very sympathetic to a jury. I've seem women go absolutely crazy when a cop knocked on their door in the middle of the night and told them they had found their husband murdered. It's been a little easier ever since we started sending a female officer along but not by much. She makes sense and I think a jury would buy it."

They turned back to the monitor as Will asked his next question.

"Mrs. Jefferson, we found your fingerprints on the pen, the murder weapon."

"I'm not surprised" the now agitated widow bristled. "I don't know if you're married, but in our home I do the laundry and all the cleaning and I have probably taken that pen out of Peter's shirt pocket a hundred times. He never hung anything up and would throw his dirty shirt on the floor at the foot of the bed. He always left his damned pen and phone book in his pocket. Of course it would be covered with my fingerprints. I'd be surprised if it wasn't." She seemed upset at what she considered a stupid and insulting question.

The Chief turned back to Collin. "If you sat on a jury, would you have some reasonable doubt about her being guilty?"

"I'd have a lot of doubt, yes, but she's the only one with a real motive, the opportunity and no alibi. I'd have doubts, sure, but I still think she did it."

"Do you think you could prove it to eleven other people sitting on that jury with you?" the Chief asked quite seriously.

"No, I don't think so" Collin admitted.

"I don't think anyone could" the Chief said. "This lady is not going to break down and confess like a perp at the fifty-five minute mark of an hour long TV detective show. I think you have your work cut out for you here.

"Now this other guy, the steel worker with the wife who was jumping the victim, tell Will to go after him, as well as this woman, they both seem like good prospects" and he turned and barged from the tiny viewing room, leaving Collin alone to watch the questioning.

Will's questions now took a much more personnel turn, asking Mrs. Jefferson questions she neither expected nor appreciated. His next one certainly touched a nerve. "Did you ever have any suspicion your husband may have been unfaithful to you?"

It was her first display of any real emotion as she glared at Will and took a deep breath before she answered, her voice less controlled, her hands shaking as she spoke.

"Every woman at some time in her marriage suspects her husband of playing around a little. What with the constant barrage of breasts and backsides shoved in a man's face day in and day out, it's a wonder more don't stray."

"Bus shelters have giant posters advertising Victoria's Secret that certainly leave nothing to the imagination. You ask him to pick up a loaf of bread and while standing at the checkout there's an array of magazines with a half-naked Kim something or a provocative Pam flashing her flesh. Waitresses are trained to pay special attention to the men when couples dine out and I'm sure they're taught to lean forward when serving so he can see inside their loose blouse. Yes Detective Deas, like many wives, I too have thought it could happen to a bright, handsome man like my husband. Yes, I thought it could happen and no, I don't know if it ever did." Her voice was quivering now and she was close to tears.

"Did you know your husband had a couple of credit cards in his name and the address on them was a postal box, not your home?"

"That can't be. We only have one credit card account, from a bank and we both use it. In fact I make all the payments on it. You must be wrong." She was back in control now, able to appear calm.

"Had your husband given you any jewelry lately?" Will pushed.

"What kind of jewelry? You mean a ring, or earrings, that type of thing?" she gasped.

"No, I mean a gold chain. I think it's called an ankle bracelet or slave bracelet, you know, the kind a man would give a special lady." Will was deliberately trying to upset her.

"No way, Peter wasn't that kind of man. He never bought jewelry, not for Christmas, birthdays or anniversaries. The last piece of jewelry he purchased was my wedding ring, and I helped him pick it out." Will felt he had hit a nerve on this matter.

"Well we know he purchased an expensive gold chain four weeks ago and paid for it with his credit card. Let's see" he consulted his notes. "It was three hundred and thirty-eight dollars plus tax from Imperial Jewelers on James Street north. You say you didn't get anything like that from him." He waited to see how she would react.

"I did not" she thundered.

"That's strange, we'll have to check that out" and he made a note.

"Not so strange" Mrs. Jefferson said. "People are always stealing other people's identities, something like that." She was back under control again and calmly waited for the next question.

The interrogation went on for another thirty minutes but Will knew he was spinning his wheels. Finally, he ended it by politely thanking her and directing the attending officer to take her home.

By the time she was halfway there Collin had a new search warrant on his desk for that very same household in Dundas. He and Will both agreed that if there was any evidence of use in a courtroom, it would be there.

Chapter Thirty Seven

"She's a tough one, isn't she?" Collin smiled ruefully as Will accepted the search warrant offered by his boss.

"As tough as any I've ever run up against and well prepared too. She never missed a beat on that gold chain thing and had a perfect answer for everything. You'd think she was reading from a book."

"Well, I guess she did read a lot of them over the years." Collin was still smiling. "Didn't she say she read all the new books presented to her husband for publication? Tell me, after that interview, are you still sure she did it?"

"More than ever, I may have had some reservations at the start but now, I'd bet my badge on it."

"Can you prove it? The Chief says you can't."

"At this point he's right. There's not a chance unless this" and he waved the search warrant "provides some substantial evidence. We haven't enough to arrest her let alone come close to a conviction." Will was firm, knowing from experience what would fly for a jury and what wouldn't.

"How are the other angles working out?"

Will glanced at his notebook before answering.

"I have Natasha and Lou working on Vasco the steelworker to verify all the details of his story, but unless anything comes up, I think he's a dead end. Natasha thinks Vasco did it. He's a heavy drinking brute who fits the pattern of the cheated husband but he was working the night the publisher died, so I think he's a no show. By the way, she has all the makings of a very good detective someday, very sharp.

"I asked her to check the drive time from the steel mill to the bar and back, just to make sure he could have had the time. Then I asked her to get in some civvies and walk from the Jefferson house to the bar and back. It's a small thing but it will add to the pile should we move on the Mrs."

"I also want the details on the concert Jefferson's son Leonard went to in Toronto and with whom, and I want confirmation on the details of the daughter's sleepover. We can do both while we're searching the house. If there is a lie hidden in her story, it may help to unravel the whole thing" explained Will.

Referring to his notes again Will told Collin "There are a bunch of little details to take care of, like taking his desktop, her laptop and all their phones in for a check. We also want to see if she has something she could have used to belt him with. I'm sure she did it and I'm sure if I keep looking I'll find the key but in the meantime, it's business as usual."

"There's a lot going on and it will all be in my report and if we come up dry, at least the chief will know we gave the bushes a real good beating."

"Enough already" Collin said as he held up his hand. "You appear to have it well under control. I called earlier and arranged for a crew to help you out at the house so if they're ready, you'd better be on your way" and he stood and walked around his desk.

"We could use a win on this one Will. I've had a few calls in the past few days and if you need anything just holler. The Chief and I watched her answer some of your questions and I have the same feeling about her as you. I know her husband was a skunk and quite likely deserved what he got, but we don't look good when we can't catch the bad guys" and he gave Will a pat on the shoulder as he opened his office door. "Use some of that Scottish brain power you're always on about" and he grinned as Will walked out.

Chapter Thirty Eight

The search of the Jefferson home took all day and Will was there right from the start supervising every aspect.

They collected the Crafty Press computer, Mrs. Jefferson's own laptop along with her son's computer and then gathered up all of their cell phones. This last action caused a great deal of consternation which diminished into incessant moaning and wailing about how the youngsters would be out of touch with the real world. When Will suggested to the son he should try the land line telephone all he got was a look of complete disdain. Notwithstanding the ruckus, all the items were packaged and shipped to the station for examination while the search continued.

Three officers sat in the victim's small office at the back of the house next to the kitchen sorting through papers from his desk, the floor, the top of his computer and any other flat surface in the room. By the time they had finished their systematic search of his bookcase and a pile of banker's boxes stacked in the corner, they knew all there was to know about the life and business dealings of Peter Jefferson.

The kitchen held special interest for Will Deas and Lou and they helped the forensic team in that room.

During the whole process Mrs. Jefferson sat quietly on her new sofa in the freshly painted living room thumbing through a stack of magazines on her new coffee table. The only acknowledgment regarding what was happening around her were two questions directed at Will. She asked if the police officers doing the search would clean up the mess they made when they were finished, and when would they get their electronic devices back. Other than that, she acted as though it was an everyday occurrence having her home probed and poked by police officers.

When they finished around six o'clock, Will was exhausted and wanted nothing more than a hot shower and a soft bed but he knew a long phone call was in order to bring Collin up to speed. Will knew Collin had a meeting in the morning with the Chief and the Mayor, and if he went into it without the latest information there would be trouble.

Dragging himself out to his car and giving Lou a wave as he headed home, Will slid behind the wheel and pulled out his phone.

Collin answered after one ring.

"How did it go" he asked.

"Not good" Will said, slumping into his car seat "not good at all."

"Nothing there?"

"Well what the hell are we looking for?" Will asked. "We already have the murder weapon. It was the victim's pen. We know he was whacked on the head with something flat but we don't know what. Natasha jokingly said if she was married and caught her husband fooling around with another woman, she would belt him with a frying pan. I thought she might be onto something so we went through all the cooking utensils and found three frying pans, all large enough to knock you silly and all spotlessly clean. We took them anyway. We even searched for the ankle bracelet but found nothing. She had almost no jewelry so I guess he didn't buy it for her."

"We took all the electronics and phones but again, it's a long shot. I think we've drawn a blank on this one" Will sounded depressed.

"I guess I have little to tell the boss in the morning" Collin said.

"Not unless the lab finds something on the computers but that's going to take a couple of days and to tell you the truth, I don't think they'll find anything. I guess you'll just have to tell him we're still working on it."

"You still think she did it, don't you?"

"Yes boss, I do."

"Well keep at it and leave the higher ups to me. What are your plans for now?"

"As I told you this morning, there's a dozen little things to clean up."

"Well go home, make yourself a drink and go to bed. You deserve a rest and I'll talk to you in the morning after my meeting with the brass."

"I'll take that as an order" Will said and hung up thinking the drink bit and the bed sounded perfect.

Chapter Thirty Nine

For three days Will, Lou and Natasha worked twelve to fourteen hour shifts sorting through the pile of evidence garnered during the investigation. One by one they eliminated each item on their lists as close examination proved them to be either true or false.

The concert young Leonard Jefferson was supposed to have attended in Toronto was actually in the Arts Center in Mississauga and included several bands with weird names, none familiar to the three police officers. When they found out what type of music the groups played, they hoped they would never hear of them or their music again.

The sleep-over Leonard's younger sister went to was just that, a gaggle of preteens giggling all night in the basement of a neighbor's home five doors up the street.

The computers and cell phones proved to be clean. Nothing was on them to indicate a plot, conspiracy or plan of any kind. They were returned three days after the search with thanks.

Although Mrs. Jefferson was the prime suspect, ancillary work was still being done regarding Alex Vasco, Pommeroy, and the boys on Railway Street. Two other cuckolded husbands were also eliminated as suspects when they learned one was on crutches recovering from a knee replacement and the other was in Birmingham Alabama attending his daughter's college graduation.

Both Lou and Natasha were a little discouraged at the lack of results as their research kept running into blank walls. Will found he had to continually remind them that a dead end could be a good thing because it freed them up to look somewhere else.

During this time Natasha came across a discrepancy in the report from the steel mill regarding the timing of the roll change. Mr. Vasco stated he had worked on the cobbled steel from the mill starting from the time he had arrived at eleven p.m. A cursory check with the mill verified there had been a roll change that night and there had been several strips of steel damaged necessitating them being cut up.

Bringing the report to Lou's attention she pointed out that the roll change had started at eleven thirty and the mill didn't go back into production until three twenty one a.m. After discussing it with Will, they decided that Mr. Alex Vasco had told them a whopper and further questioning was due. The two young detectives were instructed to bring him in.

Natasha called Alex Vasco and invited him to the station for some further clarification of his activities and he agreed to come in that afternoon. Will told them to do the questioning and report back to him.

He was now holding regular meetings each day with the Crown Attorney, who was the man slated to lead the prosecution effort should they finally arrest someone. He was the person who analyzed the evidence and he decided if there was a viable case against the suspect. If he thought there was little or no chance of getting a conviction, there would be no arrest and no prosecution, and at this point, that seemed to be the situation.

Will was frustrated at their inability to put a case together, Natasha was upset because someone might get away with murder, and Collin Fraser was agitated because the Mayor and the Chief kept calling him wanting to know when an arrest would occur. None were very happy at the prospects of having nothing to offer on the day of the big meeting in the conference room at the station. The team needed a break.

Alex Vasco walked into the station at the appointed time and seemed in a good mood as Natasha escorted him to the interrogation room. He never took his eyes off her as she set up a tape recorder and microphones between them and smiled at her whenever she looked his way. When this was done she nodded to Lou and he started the questioning.

"Mr. Vasco, do you know a man named Peter Jefferson? This man" and Lou slid a formal picture of the victim across to the steel worker.

"You mean the guy who was killed in an alley several days ago? The one who's been in the papers and on TV all week? No, I can't say as I do" was his answer.

"Are you sure? Look closely please."

"No, I've never seen this man before except from the news."

"We think your wife knew him quite well" Natasha offered.

Mr. Vasco sat still as a statue, the only sign he was conscious being the throb of a vein in his neck. He didn't blink nor breathe, just sat staring at them for what seemed a long time. Finally he spoke.

"I don't know what you're talking about" he said.

"We'll get to that in greater detail in a few moments, but first we want to ask you about your activities on the evening Mr. Jefferson was murdered. Could you tell us again exactly when you started, what the work was, and when you took your breaks?"

Alex Vasco repeated all he had told them before in his home. As he spoke Natasha followed her notes from that conversation, nodding to Lou that there was little if any difference between the two descriptions of the evening's events in the rolling mill.

"Mr. Vasco, we've been going over the time sheets from the mill and have come up with a somewhat different story than you have just told us" Lou stated.

"How's that?" the big man demanded.

"Before we go any further, I should read you a caution regarding anything you may say" and Lou read from a sheet in front of him then asked "Do you want to get a lawyer to be with you during the balance of this meeting?"

"No, I've done nothing illegal and I don't need any damn lawyer. Ask away all you like." Alex was angry.

"Very well Mr. Vasco. You said there was trouble in the mill and you worked steadily from first arriving until your shift finished. Is that correct?"

"That's correct."

"The mill's documents tell a different story. They show that the roll change started at eleven thirty P.M. and finished at three-seventeen A.M. That would suggest there was no work for you from your start time until the first strip came down the table rolls, shortly after three o'clock. We've talked to the mill superintendent and several of your fellow workers and none of them remember seeing you at any time before three a.m. Can you explain that?"

"No I can't. I was there. They just don't remember. The super would have been busy, hardly concerned with the whereabouts of a lowly Burner at the bottom end of the mill. Check my time card. I punched in just before eleven and went to my post. There was nothing to do so I may have found a spot for a cat-nap. We often do that."

"Let's get back to your wife Lindsey" Lou changed the subject and Vasco once again seemed to freeze up. "We have credible evidence that she knew the victim very well" Lou was being as careful with his wording as he could.

"I know nothing about that" Vasco said quietly.

"Well we do, and I can assure you they have been friends for a long time, and we think you knew about their friendship."

"What if I did, so what? Lindsey and I have a pretty open marriage. If you're suggesting she was fooling around with this dead book guy and it was me who whacked him, you're both nuts. I've never heard anything so stupid." He came close to laughing as he spit out his words.

Natasha jumped in here "It's not stupid Mr. Vasco. Many murders have been committed by a spouse who discovered their partner was being unfaithful. It's not unusual at all, and you can't account for four hours right at the time of the murder. Now why don't you be honest and tell us what you were doing between eleven and three that evening."

The big steelworker seemed to slump deeper into his chair, both shoulders sagging as all his bravado seemed to slip away. He appeared a lesser man than he did only minutes before. Minutes passed as he slowly looked from Natasha to Lou and back. They could almost hear his brain working. They were sure they had their killer, and he was about to confess.

Alex Vasco finally took a deep breath and leaned forward. "I was with another woman."

"I beg your pardon" Lou sputtered.

"You heard me. I was with another woman that night. I came in and saw the scheduled roll change, knew how long it would take, and called my friend.

She was happy to hear from me, hopped into her car and was at the mill side door to pick me up within fifteen minutes. Her husband was out of town so she took me home. I was back in the mill by quarter after two. We do it all the time and nobody really cares."

Lou looked at Natasha and she just rolled her eyes. If this checked out, it was another dead end.

"Tell me about this woman you visited." Lou asked.

"She's married and her husband is a prominent lawyer in town and if this ever gets out, it would cause a lot of trouble."

"We will need all the details about you and this lady, how you left the steel mill, and where you met her. We will have to get a statement from her but we can be discreet. It's not our intention to cause family breakups. There is no need to let this go beyond you, her and my partner and I, so I would suggest you not worry about this getting out if you are honest and all the details check out."

Lou pulled a small stack of blank paper from his briefcase and shoved it across the table toward Vasco.

"Please write all the facts down. I want you to include names, addresses, motels and times. Leave nothing out. If we find one error or one lie, we'll bring her in for questioning and it won't be a secret anymore" and said as he stood up.

"One of us will be back in five minutes for your statement and information and then this meeting is over. We have to step outside for some fresh air"

Chapter Forty

Collin set the time for a meeting with Will and his team so they could thrash out where they were going on the case. These usually occurred in Collin's office but this time he told them to be in the boardroom at nine the next morning. Will considered this a little odd but when he, Lou and Natasha entered the room, he knew why the change of venue.

Sitting with their backs to the entrance door were Collin, The Chief and the recognizable tall figure of Herman Duchek, Hamilton's senior Crown Attorney, called by some 'The Undertaker' because he always wore black on his skinny frame and no one had ever seen a smile cross his bleak face.

Will knew with the presence of The Chief and The Undertaker at any meeting indicated it was serious, so he reminded himself not to be flippant or smart assed when answering questions.

He, Lou and Natasha took seats across from Collin, The Chief and Duchek and placed their papers on the long table, ready for things to get underway.

The Chief spoke first.

"Tell me what's happening and where the hell we are going on this damn thing." He was never one for flowery speeches or normal social niceties like 'hello' or 'how are you'.

Collin nodded at Will to get started with his report.

"Well Sir" opened Will, "as you can see from the extensive report we sent to you and Chief of Detectives Fraser and Mr. Duchek, we seem to be going nowhere.

"Why not?" barked the Chief.

"We haven't enough courtroom evidence for any kind of a credible prosecution. Mr. Duchek has worked closely with us on this matter over the past several days and he certainly is known as one of the best Crowns in Ontario. He feels we would be laughed out of court by a second rate law student if we went ahead and charged our prime suspect and brought her before a judge and jury.

"That's the wife you're referring too, isn't it?" another bark.

"Yes Sir, she's our prime suspect."

"Herman, you've read the report, do you concur with what Deas is saying?" demanded the Chief.

"Yes sir, Detective Deas is right. He's an excellent investigator and he and his team have worked hard on this. I find no fault or short comings in his search for evidence and I think he's right in his suspicions but we can't prove it and we're going nowhere on this.

"It would make the force look foolish if we moved on it. Some might even say you were forced by the Mayor to make an arrest, you know with the elections only eight months away." The Undertaker was working The Chief the way he worked a jury in a courtroom.

225

The Chief nodded and said to them all "We can't have the police looking like fools. Our job is hard enough to do without people snickering at us behind our backs. And we don't want some smarmy twit of a newspaper writer suggesting we would bend to political pressure. I'll be damned if we have that." Turning to his right he asked "Do you agree with all this Collin?"

"I do. You know how much I hate to admit we've been stumped and can't collect enough evidence to arrest someone and send them to trial. But in this case I think Will and Herman are right, there's no way we can make this stick to anyone.

"We have the weapon but we'll never prove who stuck it into him. We don't know what he was hit with and probably will never know. As for motive, hell we have suspects all over the place so any defender can easily shift the blame.

"The only thing we might have is where his watch and the contents of his pockets went, but that might not show up for years, if ever. I think this one has gone cold and we should stop banging our head against a wall."

The Chief looked at all sitting around him. "Okay then, here's what we do. Collin, set up a press conference for late Friday afternoon. Make sure all the press, in town and out, get the call. I'll be there as support and you Deas, you be there too, and bring your team with you.

"Collin, try to come up with some story line about how this is one of the toughest investigations we've run up against in a long time and how it will take much longer etc. etc., blah blah blah. You know what I mean. Make it a good one and call me Thursday with the details so I'm up to speed." He looked again at the small group present, but they just sat silent.

"What the hell" he finally said. "We can't win them all and this may just be one of the rare ones that get away" and he stood, head and shoulders above all of them as they rose with him. Without another word The Chief turned toward the door but only made it as far as the threshold before stopping and turning back to Collin.

"And by the way, since we're not going to arrest that woman, cut her loose and leave her alone. She's still a suspect in a case we haven't solved, but we have to leave her alone for the time being. This one can go into the cold case file and we'll keep an eye on it, but I don't want a constant hassle going on with her. We don't need a harassment suit against us" and then he did leave, plowing his way through the doorway and out of the room like a Clydesdale.

Chapter Forty One

Later that day, Will invited Lou and Natasha back to his place for drinks to chat about the case and the upcoming press conference. He had an earlier dinner with Collin to go over details of the news release and he wanted to bring them up to speed. They showed up about eight and before long all were relaxing quietly in Will's den with drinks in hand. Sherlock, Will's cat, deemed the two newcomers to be intruders and sticking his tail in the air, haughtily left the room.

Natasha started the discussion with the first comment directed at Will.

"Do you really think she did it?"

"Without any doubt" Will said.

"And we're not going to arrest her?"

"No, not now anyway, we're not."

"Then she gets away with murder" Natasha stated emphatically.

"For now, if she did it, yes, but remember there's no such thing as a Statute of Limitations on murder. If new evidence comes to light or a credible witness steps forward next week, next year, or even twenty years down the road, she could be arrested, tried and if convicted, thrown into jail." Will took a long sip of his Scotch.

"But I thought we were supposed to identify the wrongdoer, take them into custody and let the system handle it from there. Here we're acting like judge and jury as well." Natasha was not happy.

"Well first off, we are part of the system you talk about. We're not isolated from the justice system, we're part of it" he stopped for a second to let that sink in.

"The problem we have here is that the law-and we are servants of that law-says she is innocent until proven guilty to a jury of her peers. If you or I cannot prove she is guilty of murder, she has not gotten away with anything, she is innocent.".

Will continued "She's the sympathetic victim of a crude and nasty philanderer and her defense would use every trick in the book to get her off. For all we know they'd probably prove he slapped his wife and children around in the past because from my notes he seemed like that kind of guy. If you arrest someone knowing you can't convict them, and the Crown knows he can't win, and when she's acquitted and she walks, all you've done is bring discredit to the force, cost the taxpayers a bundle and ruined the lives of her two children. On top of that, you can't try her again for the crime if new evidence was to surface. What have you gained? Not much and when you're finished, he's still dead." Will was on a roll.

"A lot of people are genuinely happy he's dead and the three lives he made miserable for a long time are moving ahead into a much brighter future. I don't know about you but I think we have done the job the system requires of us." Again Will took a long sip of his drink.

Natasha wouldn't let it go. "We swear to uphold the law. We hold a Bible in our hand and take an oath to enforce the law, what about that oath?" she almost yelled as Will set his drink down and turned fully to face her.

"You are absolutely right. We do take an oath to uphold the law and that means to uphold all the laws, not just the ones we like or agree with. The law says you are innocent until decreed guilty by twelve of your peers, not by a small group of detectives on your police force, or a gaggle of newspaper reporters or radio commentators. You are innocent until proven otherwise to your peers in a court of law, and peers mean everyday people like the accused. Somewhere along the line, the discretion of all those involved must come into play."

"The only thing between us and robots is discretion. The laws say the speed limit on our highways is a hundred kilometers per hour. When was the last time you heard of someone getting a ticket for going one hundred and five, or even one hundred and ten? Are not those people breaking the law?" he asked.

"What about when you're called out after midnight to quell a noisy house party? Do you just barge in and arrest everyone for disturbing the peace? No. You tell them to pipe down and if they don't, you'll be back with the Paddy Wagon. Their neighbors didn't call the police because they wanted the rowdies thrown in jail. They wanted them to shut the hell up so their neighbors on the block could get some sleep. Those noise makers broke the law but discretion is what separates us from machines and monkeys."

"If there is no humanity, no discretion, no sense of fair play, the cop becomes the enemy. The police become not the protectors of the people but the imposers of rules established by temporary holders of public office. And those rule-makers sometimes can't see what unknown consequences can occur over the years. Please be careful when standing firm on who did what and to whom."

Will wanted the girl to understand because she was a good cop and could go a long way but she had to temper what she did and thought with common sense.

"Constable Iannini, a long time ago I walked a beat for ten years with a grizzled old Irish cop. He scared the hell out of me but he was respected, feared and even loved by the people on the streets. He could have, on any given day, arrested half the people on his beat for some crime or another, but didn't."

"Prostitutes who minded their P's and Q's were left alone because he felt they provided a service to lonely old men and probably kept innocent young girls from being bothered."

"Bootleggers were another group of lawbreakers who provided a service. He used to claim politicians made laws banning liquor sales on Sunday then sent their chauffeurs out on Saturday to pick up their Sunday booze. He believed he was out on the streets to preserve the peace, not to tell people how to live their lives. And you know, he did preserve the peace, and it was a quiet, law abiding time."

"Mrs. Jefferson may very well have killed Peter Jefferson and we may never be able to prove it because all we have are suspicions. Did she find the secret section in his computer? How would you prove that? Did anyone see her slip out of the house, fry pan in hand, the night of the murder? We've already canvassed the neighbors and none of them saw anything. You could never prove she hit him with that pan and if you could, which one did she use, there are three hanging in her kitchen!"

"Her explanation that her dad is helping out is sound because Lou talked to the father and he confirmed the story. The story about the bank account works as well and you will never prove she gained entry to his computer and discovered all his nasty shenanigans with assorted women. Arresting her would just make us look like fools." Will stopped for breath.

"Then she really did get away with murder" Natasha said in wonder.

"If you truly believe that, please tell me what you would do to correct the situation. Should the state, through its police force, be able to arrest her on your say so, take her from her home and put her in jail because you are so damn sure she killed someone?"

"It has taken over a thousand years to reach this point in our judicial system and although no one will ever say the system is perfect, it's as good as any in the world. We should fight to defend it and no one should be able to change it just because they are sure of something. Many innocent people have gone to jail because one person has been positive of their guilt, so Mrs. Jefferson is not a killer until you prove it beyond a reasonable doubt to twelve ordinary people."

"If we are unable to prove she is a killer, than she is not a killer, and if that means once in a while a guilty person goes free, so be it. We're not perfect." It was time for another sip before he finished.

"Remember, Babe Ruth couldn't hit a home run every time he went to the plate, and we won't solve every murder that comes our way. But don't worry, with you and Lou working on it, we're sure to get the next one" Will said with a wink.

Natasha sat quietly, looking back at the old detective with a quizzical look on her face.

"Babe who?" she asked.

The Last Chapter

Lou and Natasha announced their engagement almost six months after the big meeting with the Chief. The search for the killer in the violent death of Peter Jefferson was officially designated a case unsolved but still under investigation and shifted to another unit.

The not very surprising announcement by the two young police officers triggered Natasha's immediate transfer out of the Homicide Division to the Social Relations Section because the rules were very clear, they could not work together in the same division. Will was pleased about their engagement, but hated losing her.

Their marriage was a glorious affair on a sun soaked Saturday morning at the splendidly located Basilica of Christ the King in Hamilton's west end. As expected, the bride was stunningly beautiful in white and the groom nervous in black, as she made her way down the isle with her father.

After the ceremony they made their way through the cathedral's huge doors and down the wide stairs beneath the lances of their honor guard of twenty-four meticulously uniformed police officers. With over half the force present, it was a grand affair.

Will arrived formally decked out in his best Cameron kilt complete with sporran, and a sgian dubh in his sock, moving about in his ghillie brogues, shaking hands and slapping backs, causing any stranger to think he was the father of the beautiful bride.

The reception was another grand affair with much laughter, bawdy jokes and incessant glass tinkling to make the bride and groom stand and kiss at least a couple of dozen times. Although the young couple left early, the party ran on into the wee hours, and quite possibly resulted in the highest percentage of inebriated Hamilton Police officers in one place at one time in the city's history.

The next morning the happy young couple's limousine had an escort from their hotel to Toronto's Pearson Airport. Amid much laughter the couple's car was led by three gleaming police cars with lights flashing and sirens wailing. Another three brought up the rear trying to out-noise and out-flash the leaders. This carried on all the way along the Queen Elizabeth Highway to the departures level at the airport and anyone who witnessed it is probably still wondering whether they saw some member of the royal family, or an entertainment giant, leaving town that day.

The Chief, to his credit, had asked the Mayor to see what could be done for the pair and as a result Lou and Natasha flew to their honeymoon in Freeport Bahamas in the First Class section, pampered by doting flight attendants who thought they were cute.

They got off the plane just a little tipsy from the champagne served non-stop throughout the flight and climbed cheerily into the horse drawn carriage provided by the resort they would be staying at. Both giggled all the way to the hotel.

It was an idyllic week with sun and sand during the day and soft breezes under the stars at night. They laughed about the weight they would gain while wading through the long buffets of food and happily washed it all down with a concoction of rum and fruit juices that tasted a little different each time a new batch was made. It didn't matter, they loved every moment they were awake.

Near the end of their week Lou rented a small Vespa scooter for a day so they could get off the resort grounds and explore some of their honeymoon island.

With much laughter they left the worried looking rental agent at the curb wondering if the two young Canadians knew what they were doing as they bounced and jerked their way out onto the Levarity Highway and headed northwest.

They dawdled through little towns and villages with names like Wild Goose Town and Bain Town until they found themselves alone in the wide open spaces covered with only low lying scrub swept clean by centuries of hurricanes. The two happy explorers made their way toward the village of West End where the island ended. Cruising around the old resort next to an abandoned airstrip, they found a secluded cove away from prying eyes and took a quick dip to cool off. An hour later they reluctantly decided it was time to head back.

Beside the road back to Freeport just south of West End stood a weathered old sign with a faded white arrow pointing toward the beach and a place called Harry's American Bar. Natasha squeezed Lou's arm and pointed at the sign so he turned onto the gravel roadway. In no time they were off the scooter and walking the tropical flowered path to the entrance of an extraordinary old Harry's American Bar.

The place sat right on the beach and looked to have been there at least a hundred years. The weathered wooden door had no handle or lock as they pushed inside. It took several seconds for their eyes to adjust to the low light seeping through the small windows spotted haphazardly around the room.

A young Bahamian waitress asked if they wanted in or out and they said out, overlooking the beach, so she walked them across the creaky old wooden floor toward a wide open back. On their right was a long bar with nautical maps of the Bahamas Islands under the bar's glass cover and the chairs and barstools looked like they had been salvaged from the wrecks of ancient sailing vessels. The place reeked of character and looked like it had seen more hurricanes than honeymooners over its long life. The young couple immediately fell in love with everything about the place.

With a tall cool drink in hand they lingered on the deck overlooking the warm waters and soaked up the late afternoon sun. Surrounded by walls and furniture that almost spoke to them of the many things they had seen, Harry's was the most perfect spot on the planet to end their honeymoon.

After an hour of almost silent dreaming and hand holding they reluctantly decided it was time to drink up and head back to the hotel. The young Bahamian brought their bill and Lou took his new wife's hand as the two of them walked to the front so he could pay. A lady with a beautiful tan across her bare back and shoulders standing at the cash register turned toward them and smiled, her brightly colored off the shoulder blouse revealing her tan to be even and unbroken.

"Hello Detective Schatz, and you Constable, how nice to see you again" she smiled with genuine warmth. "It's truly a pleasant surprise to have you drop into my little place" and she reached over the counter and took Natasha's left hand.

"My goodness, what a beautiful ring, did he pick it out himself? He did? How wonderful, I always thought you two would make a beautiful couple. I'm so happy for you" and she took the bill from Lou's hand and crumbled it up, tossing it into a waste bin.

"I hope everything was satisfactory and you enjoyed your visit. Please, put your money away and call the drinks a tiny belated wedding present, and take my best wishes with you."

They left moments later, still in a state of shock, mouths open and in stunned silence, unable to get over how wonderful and young and happy the widow Jefferson looked.

CPSIA information can be obtained at www.ICGtesting.com
Printed in the USA
BVOW05s1004240715

409645BV00004B/12/P

9 780987 864833